W9-BFG-090

RUNNING ON THE CRACKS

RUNNING ON THE CRACKS

Playscript written by Andy Arnold

based on the novel *Running on the Cracks*
written by Julia Donaldson

OBERON BOOKS
LONDON

WWW.OBERONBOOKS.COM

First published in 2016 by Oberon Books Ltd
521 Caledonian Road, London N7 9RH
Tel: +44 (0) 20 7607 3637 / Fax: +44 (0) 20 7607 3629
e-mail: info@oberonbooks.com
www.oberonbooks.com

Copyright © Julia Donaldson and Andy Arnold, 2016

Julia Donaldson and Andy Arnold are hereby identified as authors
of this play in accordance with section 77 of the Copyright, Designs
and Patents Act 1988. The authors have asserted their moral rights.

All rights whatsoever in this play are strictly reserved and
application for performance etc. should be made before
commencement of rehearsal to Caroline Sheldon Literary Agency
Ltd, 71 Hillgate Pl, London W8 7SS. No performance may be
given unless a licence has been obtained, and no alterations may
be made in the title or the text of the play without the author's
prior written consent.

You may not copy, store, distribute, transmit, reproduce or
otherwise make available this publication (or any part of it) in
any form, or binding or by any means (print, electronic, digital,
optical, mechanical, photocopying, recording or otherwise),
without the prior written permission of the publisher. Any person
who does any unauthorized act in relation to this publication may
be liable to criminal prosecution and civil claims for damages.

A catalogue record for this book is available from the British
Library.

PB ISBN: 978-1-78319-868-9
E ISBN: 978-1-78319-869-6

Cover image by Pilot Theatre York

Printed and bound by 4edge Limited, Essex, UK.
eBook conversion by CPI Group (UK) Ltd, Croydon, CR0 4YY.

Visit www.oberonbooks.com to read more about all our books
and to buy them. You will also find features, author interviews and
news of any author events, and you can sign up for e-newsletters
so that you're always first to hear about our new releases.

Contents

Acknowledgements

Thanks to Pilot Theatre York for the front cover image.
Also thanks to Pilot Theatre York and Tron Theatre Glasgow
for the additional education pack.

CHARACTERS

Key Characters

LEO – Leonora Watts-Chan

FINLAY

FINLAY'S MUM

UNCLE JOHN – John Baldwin, Leo's uncle

AUNT SARAH – Sarah Baldwin, Leo's aunt

RAB – the newsagent

DRESSING GOWN – Mary's neighbour

MARINA

MARY MCNALLY

JIM – the nurse

THE GODFATHER

LORRAINE

MUSIC COLLEGE RECEPTIONIST

KIM YEUNG

SOCIAL WORKER

LEO'S GRANDFATHER

Minor Characters

STATION TICKET OFFICER

RADIO ANNOUNCER

CLUBBERS

CUSTOMER AT DOUGHNUT STALL

WILMA – Psychiatric patient

MAN IN STREET

OLD CHINESE MAN

OLD CHINESE WOMAN

VOICES ON PHONE, FROM OFFSTAGE

Running On The Cracks was adapted as a play from the novel of the same name by Julia Donaldson.

Andy Arnold wrote the stage adaptation and it was first produced by Pilot Theatre York together with Tron Theatre Glasgow. The first performance took place at the Tron Theatre on 6 February 2013 with the following cast:

Jessica Henwick   LEO

Suni La   KIM, MARINA, WILMA, LORRAINE, OLD WOMAN

Gaylie Runciman   MARY, FINLAY'S MUM, CLUBBER, SOCIAL WORKER

Stephen Clyde   UNCLE JOHN, GODFATHER, RAB THE NEWSAGENT, NURSE JIM, STATION TICKET OFFICER, OLD MAN, CLUBBER, MUSIC SCHOOL RECEPTIONIST, LEO'S GRANDFATHER

Grant McDonald   FINLAY

Creative Team

Katie Posner   DIRECTOR

Gem Greaves   DESIGNER

Mark Beasley   LIGHTING DESIGNER

RJ McConnell   SOUND DESIGNER

Playwright's note

When adapting a novel into a play, choices must inevitably be made. The novel, *Running On The Cracks,* has just under fifty thousand words and the play has about ten thousand words of dialogue. Unlike a film version, a play must all take place in one performance space and with a limited number of actors. Therefore, not all the characters from the novel can be represented, nor all the storylines. In this story Leo's cousin Jacqueline and even the dog, Zigger, had to be abandoned! The ending of the play is also different from that of the novel. However, in such a dramatic interpretation, the aim is always that the key characters and the essential story remain intact. It is rather that this becomes a theatrical experience over the course of an hour instead of the longer experience of reading a novel and allowing the imagination to picture all the characters and scenarios.

For the first co-production between Pilot and Tron theatres we agreed that the play could be staged with five actors and with some of them playing a number of roles.

I don't believe the play could be performed with fewer but it could certainly accommodate many more actors since there are some twenty-three characters in the play altogether.

The play has been written in a style which is aimed at making it fast-moving and with an inbuilt energy. Stage scenery should be kept simple to accommodate all the locations and enable the production to run from one scene to the next with minimal fuss. Likewise, costume changes should be kept to the bare essentials. Audiences can work out very quickly which characters are which and where they are. Many scenes are written with action and dialogue taking place simultaneously on different parts of the stage. Sometimes lines by one character cut into the lines of another. I've put a / when that happens. The dialogue is meant to be delivered in a tight economical way. The stage directions often describe moments of movement and action without dialogue. These are not set in stone but rather give an indication as to how parts of the story and some scene settings can be developed by using visual tableaux as an effective theatrical device.

Andy Arnold

SCENE ONE

Empty stage.

LEO appears in a single spotlight facing the audience.

LEO: This is the bit I've planned … I wish my hands would stop shaking.

Blackout.

Split stage: on one side LEO (in Bristol); on the other FINLAY (in Glasglow).

'Galloping Horseman' music plays, while LEO sleeps in bed. FINLAY is also sleeping.

KIM enters and walks in front of the audience with food samples.

KIM: Authentic Dim Sum! Genuine Chinese family food like in China … freshly steamed on the premises … You taste these, you'll never go to your local takeaway again!

Sound of aircraft takes over and simultaneously we see an image on the wall of a middle-aged Chinese man and his English wife in happy smiling photo – maybe with young LEO.

The photo dissolves to sound of a plane crashing – LEO wakes up screaming from a nightmare.

At the same time …

FINLAY'S MUM: Finlay!

UNCLE JOHN and AUNT SARAH are there to comfort LEO.

She falls asleep again – dark soundscape.

UNCLE JOHN and AUNT SARAH switch the light out and leave, UNCLE JOHN hovers in the doorway and goes to feed his two lemon-yellow cockatiel birds in the same room, then comes and kneels by LEO's bed. He peers up close; he is wearing thick-rimmed glasses … silhouetted in the darkness; what's he doing? LEO wakes again – repeat of nightmare scream.

FINLAY'S MUM: Finlay! Are you up yet?

UNCLE JOHN is seen peering at LEO.

UNCLE JOHN: No need to wake … Uncle's here.

FINLAY'S MUM: Finlay! You've got five minutes – this paper round was your idea, not mine.

UNCLE JOHN: Sweet dreams … how sweet you look dreaming.

FINLAY and LEO both stir.

FINLAY'S MUM: Finlay, WAKE UP!

UNCLE JOHN: Shush … shush … eyes closed … mouth … *(He peers even closer – he could almost be kissing her.)*

FINLAY: *(Bolts upright.)* It's seven o'clock! Aaargh!

LEO: *(Bolts upright – she screams – taken over by sound of train whistle.)*

Both FINLAY and LEO jump up and start running.

SCENE TWO

In newsagents.

RAB: Who's walked off with those bloody *Telegraph* supplements?

FINLAY arrives out of breath. He is wearing his school uniform but with a goth-like appearance.

FINLAY: I saw you put that pile of *Heralds* on top of them.

RAB: Ah, good afternoon Finlay. What's that black muck on your fingernails?

FINLAY: *(Faint withering sigh.)* Nail varnish.

RAB: What do they call that shade then? Black death?

FINLAY: *(Referring to the newspaper.)* … 'BODY FOUND BY BIN MAN' … don't spill ash on your *Scotsman* …

Exits.

RAB: *(Shouting after him.)* If you get any of that 'black death' on the papers you'll be the next body in the bin!

To fast-moving soundscape, FINLAY runs, pushing papers from his bag into letterboxes. Sound of doors banging.

LEO is running in her school uniform as if back from school.

Sequence stops with a single door bang – followed by ambient station sounds.

LEO: A standard day single to Paddington please …

TICKET COLLECTOR: *(Smiles weakly.)*

LEO: … I'm going to see the Dali exhibition at the Tate Britain.

Another door bang.

FINLAY is outside MARY MCNALLY's door.

LEO: *(In the station loo.)* Bit tight in here – should have gone in the disabled loo.

Silence, waiting.

Doors open and shut next to LEO – 'BANG BANG BANG', while FINLAY tries to shove paper into MARY's letterbox.

LEO: Someone coming towards me …

FINLAY: Anybody in there?

LEO: *(For a second she freezes.)* Don't be so paranoid!

FINLAY: *(Waits, curious, peers through the letterbox.)* Light's on. What's that smell?

LEO: No one's looking for me yet. *(Still in the loo, she starts to change out of her school uniform and brings other clothes out of a bag … An echoey station announcement wafts through the air.)*

FINLAY: *(As he starts to walk away he imagines the headlines out loud.)* … Hmmm, 'BODY FOUND IN FLAT … Neighbours and even the regular paper boy had failed to spot tell-tale signs.' Shit!

FINLAY goes back to MARY'S door and starts knocking.

LEO, still changing, freezes again as if someone is knocking on her door.

FINLAY: *(Peering through the letterbox.)* Hmmm, smells kind of meaty … like flesh … like decaying flesh!

Loud meow sound and FINLAY steps back and bumps into DRESSING GOWN on the landing outside MARY's flat.

DRESSING GOWN: Whit d'ye think ye're doing?

FINLAY: I was just a bit worried about Mr … Mrs … McNally.

DRESSING GOWN: MISS McNally.

FINLAY: She's not been collecting her papers. Do you think she's all right?

DRESSING GOWN: Having one of her downers, that's all. This time next week she'll be dancing 'The Dashing White Sergeant' all night long, knowing her.

FINLAY: I see. *(He doesn't really.)* Only there's this strange fleshy smell coming from/

DRESSING GOWN: /That'll be cat food wee, man. She'll neglect herself but no the moggie. Spends all her benefit on cat food, that one does.

By now LEO has finished changing into her ordinary clothes.

Station announcement:

'The 9.45 for Glasgow Central is now arriving at Platform 1. Calling at Cheltenham Spa, Birmingham New Street, Preston, Carlisle and Motherwell. Platform 1 for the 9.45 to Glasgow Central.'

LEO puts on sunglasses and leaves the loo with her uniform in her bag.

FINLAY: Cat food … okay … that sounds about /

DRESSING GOWN: *(As she walks away.)* Right, Sherlock Holmes, aren't you? Shouldn't you be at school?

LEO stops as if the remark was addressed to her. Sound of stationmaster's whistle.

FINLAY: *(Looking at his watch.)* Oh no! *(Followed by a loud sound of a train leaving the station.)*

FINLAY running on one side, LEO crouched in fast-moving train on the other. She takes biscuits out of her bag and starts eating them mechanically to the sound of the train.

SCENE THREE

Sounds of Glasgow Central Station. People moving about, LEO moving with them. Eventually sits looking stressed and tired … ignored by commuters. Possible routine of LEO sitting between two people – stealing food from one of them who's on a mobile, while the other person opens a newspaper: 'ORCHESTRA ORPHAN MISSING' is visible to the audience.

LEO slips off again, eventually stands alone looking lost. Absent-mindedly she pulls the last biscuit out of the packet and chews on it. She finds a telephone box and starts to look through the telephone directory.

LEO: *(To herself.)* Chan … Chan … goodness, loads of them. Here goes *(She dials a number.)* Hello, is that Mrs Chan?

1ST VOICE: Who's speaking?

LEO: It's … my name's Chan too. Um … I'm trying to do some research into my family tree and …

1ST VOICE: Where did you get my number?

LEO: From the phone book. It's just that …

1ST VOICE: I'm sorry, I can't help you.

She dials again.

AUTOMATED VOICE: The number you have dialed has not been recognised.

She dials again.

LEO: Hello, is that Mr Chan?

2ND VOICE: Chah twing … *(crackle crackle)* … Chan … tsiu chong *(crackle crackle).* Not here.

LEO: I'm sorry, I didn't quite catch that. I'm looking for either Mr or Mrs Chan.

2ND VOICE: Chah shing help you liu *(crackle crackle)* chong.

LEO: I'm sorry, I can't understand what you're saying.

She dials again.

LEO: Hello, I'm looking for my grandmother or my grandfather. Their name is Chan.

3RD VOICE: I don't think you've got the right number.

She dials again.

LEO: Hello, is that Mrs Chan? I'm sorry if I've got the wrong number. I'm looking for Mrs Chan who used to own a Chinese restaurant.

4TH VOICE: This not a restaurant, no.

LEO: No, I know it's not a restaurant, but I wonder if you used to work in a restaurant.

4TH VOICE: I think you got the wrong number. This not a restaurant.

LEO: Yes, I know … Hello? … Hello?

RADIO ANNOUNCER: Leonora Watts-Chan, the fifteen-year old whose musician parents were tragically killed in the June 8th 'orchestra crash', has gone missing. Leonora had been living in Bristol at the home of her mother's sister, Mrs Sarah Baldwin.

AUNT SARAH and UNCLE JOHN appear at the side of the stage – microphone in their faces.

AUNT SARAH: She seemed to have settled in so well, though of course she was devastated about losing both her parents. She got on fine with my two teenage daughters and was due to start school with them on Tuesday.

UNCLE JOHN says nothing.

RADIO ANNOUNCER: Leonora set off for the bus stop on September 10th with her two cousins, but then told them she had forgotten her P.E. kit and was going back to the house to fetch it. That was the last time anyone in the family saw her. Leonora did not appear at school, and later Mrs Baldwin found a note saying that she was going to London to see old friends.

STATION TICKET OFFICER appears.

LEO: I'll be fine.

TICKET OFFICER: I remember her because she was quite chatty, although she seemed a bit nervous too. She said she was going to visit an art gallery. I didn't ask why she wasn't at school because I didn't think it was my business.

LEO: I'll be fine. Don't worry about me I've gone back to London.

RADIO ANNOUNCER: Leonora lived in North London before her parents were killed, and it is possible that she is staying with people she knew there. However, enquiries have so far drawn a blank. Anyone who thinks they may have seen Leonora should phone Missing People, 0500 700 700.

LEO: I'll be fine, Don't worry ... *(It starts to rain. She stands staring out glumly ... checks her pockets, and finds no money left. She steps out on to street.)*

Street soundscape of voices of young people coming out of late night clubs – That's my taxi yah wee shite' ... *girl screams. Sound of scuffle. LEO looking very frightened as sounds of the night get louder.*

CLUBBER: Hey doll, want some gear?

LEO: Pardon?

CLUBBER: Eccies ... jellies.

LEO: Jelly beans?

CLUBBER: Aye, jelly beans. *(Starts laughing.)*

LEO: No thanks.

CLUBBER: Hey – wee chinkie lassie wants some sweeties. *(Puts his arm round her.)* Only kidding, hen … where you heading?

LEO: Leave me alone, will you. *(Breaks away.)*

ANOTHER VOICE: Wee lassie's running home to mammy!

LEO runs on the spot, then crouches as lights fade and the sound of heavy rain starts to develop.

SCENE FOUR

Daytime: MARINA and FINLAY are setting up a doughnut stall at the market. MARINA puts a transistor radio on a stall and turns it on. On the other side of the stage LEO sleeps under newspapers.

MARINA: *(With doughnuts.)* Doughnuts – Five for a pound! *(To FINLAY who is stuck behind a newspaper with 'ORCHESTRA ORPHAN MISSING' headline on the front.)* That's a long face for a Saturday … it may never happen.

FINLAY: It already has.

MARINA: What is it this time – school or Mum and Dad?

FINLAY: Both. It's those bloody N of Ms.

MARINA: I thought N of M was a rock band.

FINLAY: That's Eminem – an ancient rapper.

LEO starts to get up – shivering and wanders around the perimeter of the acting area, cold and hungry.

MARINA: Ah … So what is it then?

FINLAY: N of M is Notification of Misconduct. They're these slips of paper the school give you, and your parents have to sign them. Mum said if I got any more she'd stop this week's pocket money. Then I was late for school on Tuesday and got one. So I forged her signature.

MARINA: Finlay! This sounds like the slippery downward slope. Did the school swallow it?

FINLAY: Yes, but then on Wednesday one of the other paper boys was off and Rab gave me all these extra houses to do, so I was late again.

MARINA: And you got another Eminem?

FINLAY: N of M – no, but I would have. I couldn't face that, so I wrote a note from Mum saying I'd been to the dentist.

MARINA: I wouldn't have given you this job if I'd known you were such a hardened criminal.

FINLAY: Only the school went and phoned her.

MARINA: What gave you away? The handwriting, was it?

FINLAY: No, it was the Ps ... Apparently there's only one in 'apologise' and two in 'appointment'. What an effing stupid language.

MARINA: Language, Finlay.

FINLAY: That's what I just said – an effing stupid one.
So now that's the pocket money gone *and* Mum's going to stop me doing the paper round if I'm late again. I'll never get that guitar, and Ross'll probably find someone else to be in the band.

MARINA: Five for a pound! ... All this talk of 'p's ... Mind the van a minute, can you, son?

MARINA exits.

Enter CUSTOMER.

FINLAY serves customer.

FINLAY: *(Taking the twenty-pound note.)* Haven't you got anything smaller?

CUSTOMER: ... Nuh.

FINLAY: ... Hang on. *(Turns away and is about to take change out of the money tin when LEO appears from nowhere and grabs the bag of doughnuts.)*

CUSTOMER: *(Who turns too late to see her.)* Hey, where are my doughnuts?

FINLAY: Hey! *(Chase begins. Music.)*

CUSTOMER: *(Grabbing Finlay.)* Hey! Hang on! My change!

FINLAY: *(Breaking free from the CUSTOMER.)* Come here!

CUSTOMER: … FRIGGING TWENTY-POUND NOTE!

CUSTOMER chases FINLAY who chases LEO. FINLAY bangs into someone and the twenty-pound note falls out of his hand. They run full circle and crash into stalls. LEO makes her escape.

MARINA re-enters.

MARINA: Jesus Christ! What's going on?

CUSTOMER: Wee toerag ran off with my doughnuts.

FINLAY: It wasn't me – it was a girl who had your doughnuts. I was running after her.

MARINA: *(To CUSTOMER.)* Sorry about that. Here's another bag.

CUSTOMER: … and my change – frigging twenty-pound note that was …

MARINA: All right, mind your language, will you? Finlay, give the gentleman his money.

FINLAY searches his pockets.

FINLAY: I think I lost it.

MARINA: You think you lost it?

FINLAY: I must have dropped it when I fell. I was trying to catch this thief, you see.

MARINA: Ah … *(Looks in the box but there is not enough change left –she hands him a twenty-pound note.)* Compliments of the house.

CUSTOMER: Thanks. *(Sarcastic. He exits.)*

FINLAY: Thanks, Marina – I'll pay it back.

MARINA: I know you will – your next couple of weeks' wages.

MARINA starts to prepare the stall again. FINLAY says nothing but picks up the newspaper again and looks at the headline – Bingo! He starts to leave.

MARINA: Where do you think you're going? You stay right here.

FINLAY stays put.

SCENE FIVE

We are now in the park. LEO enters and sits on the bench, tired and upset, and starts to draw to calm herself. Park sounds, birdsong.

MARY enters with a large bag and takes out a huge loaf of bread to feed the birds. LEO notices all of MARY'S bread – she has only a bit of a doughnut left.

MARY laughs as she feeds birds.

LEO: *(To herself.)* Can't get the swans quite right … they still look more like geese.

MARY looks across at her.

LEO: *(Out of earshot.)* Don't come and sit here – it's my bench … any other bench in the park … they're all empty. Please don't come near me!

MARY wanders over towards LEO.

MARY: That's a nice picture … *(She sits down on a bench beside LEO.)*

Silence.

MARY: Have you got the time, hen?

LEO ignores her and keeps drawing.

MARY: Go on … gie us a swatch of yer watch.

LEO: *(Not looking at her.)* Just gone two o'clock.

MARY: Wilma'll be out for her Accompanied at half past.

LEO, bemused, says nothing.

MARY: They willnae give her Unaccompanied. The Godfather gets Unaccompanied, but Wilma jist gets Accompanied.

LEO looks longingly at the bread.

MARY: Aye, the Godfather gets Unaccompanied, but no Wilma – she'd do a runner if they gave her Unaccompanied. There's that many pubs round here. It's alcohol-induced wi' Wilma. If Wilma could stay off the bevvy she'd be as right as you are, hen. She cannae mind hersel ... too many dirty old men about.

She rummages in one of her bags and holds out a packet of biscuits to LEO.

LEO stares at them for a second. Then she takes one and hands the packet back.

MARY: Keep it, hen. I've got another one for Wilma, and one for the Godfather. Jim disnae like biscuits. I've got some crisps and juice for Jim.

They both sit, eating.

Lights up on FINLAY dialing on phone. Stage split between two scenes.

VOICE: Hello, you're through to Missing People.

FINLAY: Oh, hi ... er, I've seen the girl that's gone missing.

VOICE: Can you give us the name of the missing person, please?

FINLAY: That one in the paper.

VOICE: We do have several thousand missing people in our files. We need to work from a name.

FINLAY: I'm sorry, I can't remember. It wasn't my paper, see. I just deliver them. But it was yesterday she was in it. She's kind of Chinesy-looking.

VOICE: Do you mean Leonora Watts-Chan?

FINLAY: Aye, that was it. I'm sure it was her. She nicked a bag of doughnuts from my stall. Well, it's not my stall, really, it's /

VOICE: /Can I just take down a few details first, please?

MARY: *(To LEO.)* Whit's your name then?

VOICE: What's your name?

FINLAY: Finlay Grant.

FINLAY'S MUM: *(Off.)* Finlay!

MARY: Eh, hen?

LEO: Leo.

VOICE: And the address?

MARY: I'm a Leo … Fiery and generous, that's me.

MARY rummages in the bag, gets out a newspaper and briefly sees a glimpse of the headline: 'ORCHESTRA ORPHAN MISSING'.

MARY opens it and searches for the horoscope section.

FINLAY: 58 Tiverton Road.

VOICE: Where is that?

FINLAY: It's in Glasgow … But you won't write to me, will you? I don't want you to write. My parents don't know about this, see. I lost twenty quid when I was chasing after the girl, and I don't want them to find out. Is there a reward, by the way? I don't mind you writing to me if there's a reward.

FINLAY'S MUM: *(Off.)* Finlay – I need the phone.

FINLAY: That's my mum. I'll have to be quick.

VOICE: Can you tell me when and where you think you saw the girl?

MARY: *(Still searching.)* Where is it now?

FINLAY: Yes, it was at the Barras this morning.

VOICE: The barrows, did you say?

FINLAY: No, the Barras. It's a market. She nicked a bag of doughnuts and ran off ... heading for Glasgow Green I think.

VOICE: Can you remember what she was wearing?

FINLAY: It was some kind of anorak.

FINLAY'S MUM: Finlay – who are you talking to?

FINLAY: Just Ross, Mum.

VOICE: Can you describe it?

FINLAY: *(To phone.)* Okay, Ross, I'll be right there.

VOICE: Hello? Hello? ...

FINLAY puts down the phone.

FINLAY: *(To himself.)* Right Miss Watts ... whatever your name is ...

MARY: *(Finding horoscopes in the paper.)* Ah ... Leo ...

FINLAY: ... no hiding place for you ...

MARY: 'A chance encounter can affect your home life.'... *(Nudges LEO.)* ... A chance encounter. That willnae be Wilma. Wilma's planned. It must be you, pal!

FINLAY: *(He starts to leave.)* Can't stop, Mum! *(He stops, turns and grabs a notebook and pen, then stops again, grabs binoculars ... FINLAY the detective.)*

FINLAY'S MUM: Hang on – have you done your homework?

FINLAY exits.

Male nurse, JIM, enters with WILMA, a psychiatric patient under medication. They approach the bench.

MARY: Hiya, Jim. Move up, hen. This is the nurse, Jim, I was telling you about ... Hiya, Wilma hen. *(Offering buscuits.)*

JIM: Chocolate Hobnobs – your favourite, Wilma.

(WILMA smiles but says nothing.)

MARY: This is my new wee friend, Jim. She's a Leo like me.
Fiery and generous, aren't we, hen? Biscuits fur the Godfather,
Irn Bru and crisps fur you, Jim. *(Gives it to them.)*

JIM: You're spoiling us, Mary.

MARY: Aye, but I can afford to, Jim – I didnae spend my DLA
all at once – not like last time.

*JIM rolls his eyes at LEO. They settle down to eat biscuits in silence.
JIM notices LEO's sketchbook.*

JIM: Are you from Mary's painting class?

LEO: … Er … *(She's stuck.)*

MARY: I've stopped going to that painting class Jim. I didnae
like it. There was a wumman there kept giving me looks.

JIM: Away you go, Mary. Don't worry about other folk.
It's good for you, that class. You don't want to hang around
here all day. Tell you what, why don't you get your CPN to
find out if there's any other classes?

MARY: *(Changing the subject, turning to WILMA.)* How's the pool
going, darling? Still beating the Godfather?

WILMA nods and smiles.

MARY: You're giving her too much of they pills, Jim.

JIM: Aye … maybe so … *(Pause.)* … Let's keep moving,
Wilma. Say goodbye to Mary. *(As if he's talking to a child.
WILMA waves to MARY. They exit.)*

Pause. LEO's thinking, 'That was quick.'

MARY: Fiery and generous, that's us, hen … Leos …

Pause. MARY rummages in the bag.

LEO: *(To herself.)* CPN, DLA, accompanied, unaccompanied?
… Where have I landed?

MARY: What's that?

LEO: It's short for Leonora.

MARY: What is?

LEO: My name. It's Leonora. Mum named me after a Beethoven overture – that was so typical of her. My first bed was a spare cello case.

MARY: Yer ma played the cello then, aye?

LEO: Yes, and my dad … but they were in different orchestras. They never went on tour at the same time, so that there would always be one of them around to look after me. *(Pause.)*

There was Uncle John and Aunt Sarah in Bristol. Aunt Sarah was my mum's sister but she didn't like to help. She was a beautician and she was always immaculate-looking, with manicured fingernails and high-heeled shoes, and Mum was … well, a bit unconventional.

MARY: A bit of a tearaway, was she?

LEO: Yes, I suppose so. I think maybe Aunt Sarah disapproved of her and Dad not being married. Not as much as Dad's parents did, though. They cut him off when he moved in with Mum. *(Pause – keeping herself in check still.)* I don't think Dad ever forgave them, although he did try to explain it to me: he said that in the Chinese community anything like that was completely taboo. You didn't even go out with someone unless you were definitely going to get married.

MARY: Couldnae they get married just to please his ma and da?

LEO: That's what I sometimes think. But my dad could be quite stubborn too. Anyway, they didn't – they moved to London to join orchestras. And then they had me.

MARY: Ah well, that's /

LEO: /But then, just three months ago, Dad's orchestra was invited to Spain and they needed some extra cellos for a particular piece. It was one of Mum's favourite pieces – by some Spanish composer, for a singer and twelve cellos. I said she should go: I could stay with Aunt Sarah and Uncle John. They live in Bristol. So Mum said 'Just this once.'

MARY: And was it?

LEO: Yes … Yes, it was because the plane crashed and, well … everyone was killed.

MARY: … *(Softly.)* … Oh, hen.

Silence – broken when MARY hands her another chocolate Hobnob.

MARY: So you're the wee orchestra orphan? I read about you when it happened. *(Pause.)* What are ye doing in Glasgow?

LEO: My grandparents live here. *(Starts to get upset.)* Only, I don't know them or where they live.

MARY: You not got a number for them hen?

LEO: No. I've no idea who they are. I mean … my dad lived here … he even went to music college here … but he didn't tell me anything! …

MARY: He must have said something /

LEO: /He said they ran a Chinese restaurant in Glasgow … but there are twenty-two Chans in the phone book and I didn't pack my mobile because I thought people might somehow trace me. So I have to use phone boxes, but I keep running out of change.

MARY: Get another mobile … one o 'they smart things!

LEO: Can't afford it.

MARY: Well just go round their houses.

LEO: No.

MARY: How no? They willnae bite your head off.

LEO: It's not that. My picture was in *The Sun*.

Mary: You'll want to lie low for a wee while then.

LEO: But where? I can't afford to go and sit in cafes. My money's run out. I'm so tired, and I feel so dirty! *(Tears start to flow.)* I just want a bath!

MARY: *(Pauses. Looks at her.)* You better come back with me …
I've no got a bath mind … just a shower. Come on, help me
with these … *(Bags.)*

Music. LEO helps MARY with bags – they're heavy.

MARY: *(Sees LEO struggling.)* Cat food! *(She laughs as they exit.)*

SCENE SIX

*Soundscape. A moment of telling the story through visual images. Action
takes place in different parts of the stage: UNCLE JOHN is feeding his
yellow cockatiels; FINLAY is on the lookout and LEO is moving about
with her sketchbook looking for things to draw … Time is passing.*

UNCLE JOHN: *(To the birds.)* Here you are, nice clean water.
That's what you like, isn't it? Oh look, nasty husks – let's take
them away. Nice new seeds. Yes, you like the stripy ones, don't
you, Clemmy? Let Lemmy have some too.

FINLAY walks back home.

MARY: *(To LEO.)* Take some mair biscuits with you, hen …
you'll get hungry in the park … all that fresh air, hen.

LEO walks back to the bench to draw.

UNCLE JOHN: *(To bird but also looking in the direction of LEO on
stage.)* Who's a pretty girl, eh? You are!

FINLAY is getting ready to go out again.

FINLAY'S MUM: Where are you going now?

FINLAY: Ross's – won't be long.

UNCLE JOHN: *(To the birds.)* Don't you want to play with your
bell? Are you missing our little friend?

FINLAY'S MUM: FINLAY!

MARY: *(Back in the flat handing LEO a box of pastels.)* Mair pastels
for you, hen.

UNCLE JOHN: She'll be back. Daddy's going to find her.

Visual moment. UNCLE JOHN is feeding birds, MARY is sitting in her flat, LEO sitting on the bench drawing ... FINLAY on the lookout. He wanders into the park. LEO is sitting on her own and FINLAY is in the distance ... then he sees her ... she gets up, aware that someone is there. UNCLE JOHN is looking out as if he can see her. MARY is staring out blankly; she takes a pill. LEO gets up and starts walking, FINLAY walking behind her ... she starts running on the spot, so does FINLAY ...

RAB: Not so fast, pal! *(They both freeze.)* I've got a present for you. *(He hands newspapers to FINLAY.)*

LEO moves at the same time and bangs on MARY's door.

MARY: In you come, hen. I've just put the kettle on. We can have a wee cuppa. *(LEO enters MARY's flat.)*

FINLAY: I can't! It's not fair!

RAB: Blame it on that other wee numpty ... calling off sick all the time.

FINLAY: I'll be late for school.

RAB: Tough titty. Few more houses ...

MARY: Did you do some nice pictures, aye?

FINLAY: I'll be in trouble.

RAB: You'll be in double trouble if you don't get those papers out ... now shift it!

MARY: Where's that pussy cat gone? ... Midget!

FINLAY, now with papers, starts to run towards MARY and LEO; changes mind and runs back to his mum.

MARY: *(To LEO.)* Midget likes you, hen.

LEO: *Midget?* ... she's enormous.

MARY: Aye, but she was a wee toty thing when I found her. She was in the back court, sniffing around by the bins. All skin and bones, she was – a wee toty thing.

FINLAY: *(Back home.)* Mum! ... Mum! ... Can I borrow your camera?

FINLAY'S MUM: I'd rather you didn't.

FINLAY: I'll bring it straight back.

FINLAY'S MUM: What do you want it for?

FINLAY: Homework project ... rather complex – bye. *(Exits. He starts running. Repeat of newspaper delivery routine: doors bang.)*

SCENE SEVEN

MARY's flat.

LEO at her sketchbook.

MARY: You're a good artist. You're Leo da Vinci, you are! You like drawing birds, don't you? What are these ... wee cushie-doos?

LEO: Sorry?

MARY: Naw, they cannae be ... pigeons arenae yellow.

LEO: Oh, no ... they're lemon-yellow cockatiels. Uncle John used to keep all these birds – about twenty of them. *(Showing sketch.)* These were my favourites ... Clemmy and Lemmy.

MARY: The wee rascals. Did they talk, aye?

LEO: Not that I ever heard, but Uncle John talked to them all the time. *(Pause.)* I used to like Uncle John when I was little. I thought I did, anyway. Maybe it was his birds I liked really. He kept them in the spare room ... That was where I slept.

MARY: Eh?

LEO: The social worker sent me to live with Uncle John and Aunt Sarah when Mum and Dad died ... I slept in the spare room.

MARY: Did the birds no keep you awake?

LEO: No, because Uncle John rigged up a curtain across the cages to stop the light getting through. I liked sharing with the birds – at first, anyway. I liked sketching them. The social worker wasn't happy, though.

MARY: Are they ever?

LEO: She said it was against the law and I could get some disease off the birds.

MARY: Don't get me started about social workers …

LEO: It wasn't the social worker, it … *(Pause.)*

MARY: Go on hen … *(Pause.)*

LEO: He used to bring me in a cup of tea in the mornings, and then he'd draw the curtain across the cages to wake up the birds. This would be quite early – about seven o'clock, even earlier sometimes, but I didn't mind that. I quite liked drinking my tea in bed and watching the birds. Sometimes the tea would be a bit cold, but I just thought he'd been pottering about and had forgotten to bring it in to me – he was a bit absent-minded like that. But one morning I woke up and … he was kneeling on the floor by my bed. He was just kneeling there, leaning over me and staring at me. Usually he wears glasses, those magnifying kind, but he hadn't got them on, and his brown eyes were just inches away from my face. They looked smaller without the glasses … all watery.

MARY: Did you tell your auntie?

LEO: No. I didn't know what to say. I didn't think she'd believe me anyway. And then I started wondering if it had really happened – until it did again few days later.

MARY: Tried to mess about with you, did he?

LEO: He just knelt there staring with his little watery eyes. He just gave me this sort of soppy smile for a few seconds and then went and fetched my tea – he'd put it down on the table by the cages and it was getting cold.

MARY: What did you do – throw the tea in his face?

LEO: No. It was stupid, really – and when it kept happening, it felt too late to say anything. I suppose I should have told him to get out or something, but … well, it was his house and his room and his birds, and … Anyway, he did get out without me telling him to, but he still had that stupid soft kind of smile on his face. It was as if he was sharing a secret with me.

MARY: I'll wipe that smile off his face if I ever see him. I'll get the Godfather to wipe it off, so I will. The dirty old man.

LEO: I hope you never do see him. He thinks I'm in London. He won't come looking for me here …

Bang at the door. MARY and LEO both freeze – could this be him?

LEO creeps up to door and looks through spy hole.

LEO: Shit!

MARY: Who is it? It's no the bird man, is it?

LEO: It's that boy – he must have followed me.

MARY: What boy?

LEO: He's there outside – he's on the landing.

MARY: *(In a whisper.)* Who?

LEO: That boy … I'm sure it's him – the one I told you about, the one from the doughnut stall. Why did I come here?

MARY: We willnae let him in.

FINLAY: *(Shouting from outside the door.)* Open the door! I know you're there! Open the door or I'll call the police.

LEO: What can I do? I'm trapped.

MARY: Out of the way, hen! I'll sort him. I spy with my little eye … *(MARY looks through spy hole.)* It's my wee paper boy! Can ye no put it through the letter box, son?

FINLAY: I know she's in there.

MARY: No, wee man, there's only me – me and the moggie … no, there's nae lassie here. You've got the wrong house.

FINLAY: She *is* here! I *saw* her!

MARY: Jist gie me my *Morning Post* and stop blethering. You'll be late for school.

FINLAY: I'm not going to school. I'm going to the police station!

MARY: Aye, and I'll go with you and tell them you've been causing a breach of the peace.

LEO: You'd better let him in.

MARY opens the door and FINLAY flashes camera in LEO's face. They are on the landing at MARY's flat.

LEO: What on earth are you doing?

MARY: Is it him, aye? Is it the doughnut boy?

FINLAY: No – *she's* the doughnut *girl!* She stole my doughnuts! *(LEO grabs the camera off him.)* HEY! … and now she's got my mum's camera. *(LEO takes a photo of FINLAY.)*

MARY: Watch the birdie!

FINLAY: Give it back, you thief!

LEO: No chance – mine now.

FINLAY: Give me that camera!

Stand off … FINLAY starts to get upset.

MARY: Better give it back hen – he's feart of his maw.

LEO: He's what?

MARY: He's a wee scaredy cat. He'll get a right skelping if he loses his maw's camera.

Pause. LEO presses buttons trying to delete the photo.

LEO: That's got rid of that. Here you are, but stop spying on me.

FINLAY: I'd rather be a spy than a thief.

LEO: Stop calling me a thief!

MARY: Aye, watch your tongue, son.

FINLAY: She is one. I nearly lost my job because of you, and now I owe twenty-quid.

LEO: I don't know what you're on about. I didn't steal twenty-quid.

FINLAY: I didn't say that! … but you're still a thief. Stealing things and running away all the time. I bet that's why you ran away in the first place, isn't it? I bet you stole stuff from your aunt and uncle!

MARY: What do you mean? *I'm* her auntie.

FINLAY: You're not! You're not the one that was in the paper, anyway. I recognised you the first time I saw you, and now I'm going to get the reward.

LEO: Reward?

FINLAY: Too right.

MARY: Who have you blabbed it to you, wee eeejit?

LEO: Have you phoned the police?

FINLAY: So what if I have? You're a runaway and a thief.

LEO: Listen … you don't understand.

FINLAY: *(Shouting now.) You're* the one who doesn't understand. You just go round stealing things, not caring how other people feel. How do you think I'd feel if I lost my job? How do you think my mum would feel if her camera was stolen? My dad gave her that camera for Christmas!

MARY: Your da! Your ma! You're lucky to have a da and a ma. How d'ye think this wean feels? She's got no da and no ma – all she's got is an auntie who's a snob and an uncle who's a pervert with magni … whatsits …

LEO: Magnifying.

MARY: Aye, thick glasses *(Silence.)* … She disnae want your ma's camera. She jist disnae want her photie splashed in all the papers. But you widnae think about that, wid ye? Ye'd have her back wi' that perverted bird man, is that it?

FINLAY: What? … I didn't know …

MARY: No, and you didnae think neither. Christmas, you're on about! Christmas! What about the poor wee lassie? No ma, no da – what sort of Christmas do you think she's going to have?

DRESSING GOWN appears on the landing.

DRESSING GOWN: Is everything all right, Miss McNally?

FINLAY: *(Mutters.)* It's Dressing Gown.

MARY: Dressing Gown! Aye, *(To LEO.)* it's Dressing Gown … I'm fine, Dressing Gown! Never better! How's yerself, Dressing Gown?

DRESSING GOWN: I'll be fine if you can just keep the noise down. *(Sees FINLAY.)* I see Sherlock is back on the case. *(She hovers but gets nothing back. She finally exits.)*

MARY: Sherlock! That's good – wee Sherlock.

LEO: Sherlock Holmes had brains.

MARY: Aye, right enough.

FINLAY: I made a mistake. I'm sorry, okay?

LEO: Bit late for that!

FINLAY: Look, I won't tell anyone.

LEO: *(Turns away from him.)* You come in and sit down, Mary. Shall I make you a cup of tea?

MARY: Aye, go on – it's all through there.

LEO pauses and looks back at FINLAY.

FINLAY: I'd better go.

LEO: Yes, you'd better.

MARY: Maybe the lad wants a cuppa as well.

LEO: Mary!

FINLAY: Well …

MARY: Aye, of course he does, don't you, Sherlock ... And I know what he'll be wanting as well – Chocolate Hobnobs!

SCENE EIGHT

Music plays through a sequence of daily life: FINLAY coming and going between his own house and MARY's flat (e.g. he sits in his own house writing homework, then takes it to MARY's flat; LEO starts to help him with it. MARY hands him another biscuit, and so on). UNCLE JOHN is attending to his birds.

FINLAY'S MUM: *(On FINLAY leaving the house.)* Finlay! Where are you off to now?

FINLAY: Ross's.

FINLAY'S MUM: You've both become very pally – what's going on?

FINLAY: Not allowed to say, Mum ... secret mission. I've told you too much already ... Bye!

FINLAY'S MUM: Hey! ... Come back and finish your tea!

FINLAY starts running to soundscape. Crackly radio during this ... UNCLE JOHN listens.

RADIO ANNOUNCEMENT: Police have received a number of sightings of the missing school girl Leonora Watts Chan; however, a particular line of enquiry is that she may be in Glasgow rather than London. A spokesman said that all sightings were being explored ... *(Fades out as UNCLE JOHN turns down radio.)*

FINLAY is sitting and doing his homework in MARY's flat; LEO is painting and MARY is bringing more bags in.

FINLAY: *(To LEO.)* Are you sure you're okay about helping me again? It's just I've got a bit behind ...

LEO: I know. Too busy taking photos and catching criminals.

FINLAY: Give us a break will you?

LEO: Fine ... Where have you got up to? Has Macbeth killed the King yet?

FINLAY: Now he's just had this other guy bumped off – you know, his friend, Banquet.

MARY: Banquet! That's a good name. How do you do, Banquet? Sit doon, Banquet – have a cup of tea.

LEO: It's not Banquet, it's Banquo.

FINLAY: *(Embarrassed.)* I know … that's … er … what I said. *(Pause. He reads out his essay title.)* Is Banquo's Ghost Meant to be Real?

LEO: Well, what do you think?

FINLAY: Why shouldn't he be? Shakespeare says so. Look, it says here: 'Enter Banquo's ghost and sits in Macbeth's place.'

LEO: But don't you think that's really meant to be happening in Macbeth's mind?

MARY: Aye, like wi' Wilma on Ward 7. One time she saw this chimney-sweep talking to her oot the telly, but the telly wasnae on. There's that much funny stuff going on in people's heids.

LEO: That's right. After all, no one else can see the ghost – and remember what Lady Macbeth says: 'You look but on a chair.'

FINLAY: I suppose you always come top in English.

LEO: I never went to school actually.

FINLAY: Liar … you get arrested for that.

LEO: I was home-educated. Mum and Dad used to take me to see a lot of plays and then we'd talk and talk about them.

FINLAY: … So you think Macbeth's a bit mental then? I think that's what Lady Macbeth thinks too. She says something about how he often has these fits and how everyone should take no notice and just get on with the banquet.

MARY: Take no notice and get on wi' the banquet! That's good advice, that is! I'll tell that to Lorraine and the Godfather. Take no notice and get on wi' the banquet! Let's have a banquet. Let's get in a chinky!

FINLAY: You shouldn't say 'chinky' Mary.

MARY: Eh?

LEO: Listen, Mary, you can't keep spending your money on us like this. You've already bought me those clothes, and all those lovely oil pastels.

MARY: I've just got my DLA and I'll spend it how I like. *(She grabs a restaurant flyer by the phone.)* I'll spend it on a banquet!

MARY then starts dialing on phone.

FINLAY: *(To LEO, quietly.)* What's DLA?

LEO: Disability Living Allowance.

FINLAY: Oh …

MARY: *(On the phone.)* Hiya! Can you send roon one spare rib special, chicken balls with sweet and sour sauce, and er …

LEO: We've got to stop her.

MARY: One chicken curry with fried rice … and chips …

FINLAY: Yeah … Hey – that restaurant could be the one your gran and granddad run.

MARY: One chicken Maryland with curry sauce … and gravy …

FINLAY: *(To MARY.)* Ask them if they're called Chan!

MARY: Eh? What are you? Chans? No? Sure there's no Chans lurking in the sweet and sour? You fish them out if there are – my wee girl here is looking for her granny and grandpa.

FINLAY: *(Over MARY giving her address into phone.)* I've just had a thought there … We could order food from a different place each week, and ask each one the Chan question. That way we can track Leo's grandparents down without anyone sussing us out.

MARY: *(Putting down phone.)* Brilliant – Sherlock Holmes is on the case!

LEO: That will take ages. There must be loads of Chinese restaurants in Glasgow.

FINLAY: Let's see. *(Grabs MARY's Yellow Pages.)* R … R … Rent-a-car … Ah, here we are – Restaurants … Chinese … You're right. There's loads … at least fifty of them.

LEO: So one a week would take us about a year. I don't even know if they've still got a restaurant.

MARY: Hand over the book, Sherlock! We don't need to wait a week. Let's try this one – The Amber Wok. I bet they do a good banquet.

LEO: Mary, *no*! We're going to have far too much food as it is.

MARY: We're having a banquet! *(Sudden thought.)* We just need some mair guests.

SCENE NINE

FINLAY is walking round the set.

UNCLE JOHN: *(To the birds.)* You like it when I talk to you, don't you? Say Clemmy! Say Clever Clemmy! It was the child lock. I was going to unlock it. Don't be sad – Daddy's back now. He's got a clue. He's going to find your friend. He's going to find her before they do …

FINLAY'S MUM: Finlay? Finlay! Where is that boy now?

FINLAY arrives back at MARY's flat with Chinese food cartons.

SCENE TEN

MARY's flat. MARY is eating out of a carton and dancing to party music. Enter GODFATHER with carryout.

LEO: *(To FINLAY.)* The Godfather's just been in Ward 7 for six months. They let him out yesterday.

MARY: They've turned the key! They've set the leader free! *(Enter LORRAINE with Big Issue copies.)* Hiya doll … wee

Lorraine – newspaper girl like you, Sherlock. Watch your pockets, though – she's on the juice frae the chemist.

FINLAY: The juice?

MARY: Methadone, Sherlock.

GODFATHER: You're off yer heid, Mary.

LORRAINE: *(To LEO.)* Is this you, darling? *(Showing her the photo on front of The Big Issue.)* Got a celebrity in the house – get me oot of here! … Eh, pal?

LEO: Oh no … I don't believe it … *(Glares at FINLAY.)*

GODFATHER: Got any Buckies, Mary? *(To FINLAY.)* Fancy a wee swig of wine, pal? Done the monks nae harm.

FINLAY: Aye, maybe.

LEO: Don't you dare … you're too young to drink.

FINLAY: Shut it will you – you're not my mum.

LEO: Well, that's one blessing.

MARY: Come on – let's party! I think we'll need mair grub before long … where's that phone book?

FINLAY: Mary! You can't keep buying food for everyone. *(To LEO.)* You should cook the next banquet yourself, Leo – authentic Chinese. Like those little round things you made the other day. They were really nice.

MARY: Aye, they looked bogging but they tasted brilliant.

LEO: That's about all I can make – my dad's special Village Dumplings.

MARY: Leo's dumplings – that's right.

GODFATHER: *(To LEO.)* You're no a dumpling are you, hen? That's no nice Mary.

LEO: Anyway, what's the rush? … Mary's already bought a huge carry out.

FINLAY: Yes, but I have a feeling that this party is going to last a while.

MARY: Oh aye, you're right there, Sherlock ... spot on! It's gonna last for days ... for weeks ... months!

LEO: Well ... Okay ... but I'd have to buy the ingredients, and the only place to get them is the Chinese Supermarket.

FINLAY: Down under the motorway?

LEO: That's right ... It's got everything.

FINLAY: Come on, then ... let's go down there ... it's early doors still.

LEO: But suppose I get spotted?

MARY: They'll all be Chinkies there, hen – you'll blend in.

FINLAY: Mary!

MARY: Sorry pal. I'll get there eventually.

LORRAINE: *(Looking about, under cushions etc.)* Where's yer stash Mary?

LEO: I'm staying right here.

FINLAY: *(To LEO.)* Don't be daft ... come on.

LEO: I've got to lie low, haven't I? Thanks to you ... blabbering to the police.

FINLAY: Missing persons.

LEO: Same thing.

FINLAY: You started it – nicking my doughnuts – I could have got the sack.

LEO: Dry your eyes, will you? I'm the one in trouble, not you ... paper round ... doughnut stall ... home to Mummy. *(Starts to get upset.)*

FINLAY: What am I supposed to do? It's not my fault!

LEO: Nothing is, is it? … *(Mumbles.)* If you had a brain you'd be dangerous.

FINLAY: What?

GODFATHER comes over.

GODFATHER: Is he annoying you, sweetheart? *(Puts his arm around her.)*

LEO: *(Breaking away.)* I'm okay thanks.

MARY: *(To GODFATHER.)* She's too young for you, Godfather … Come on! Let's dance!

FINLAY: *(To LEO.)* I'm sorry … if you make me a shopping list for your Village Dumplings, I'll go on my own.

MARY: *(Now dancing with the GODFATHER.)* Aye, Sherlock can get the messages.

LORRAINE: Where're you hiding it, Mary?

FINLAY: I'll maybe go to the music college first –

LEO: What for?

FINLAY: You said your dad studied there … they might have his parents' address still.

LEO: They won't tell you anything.

FINLAY: You come with me.

LEO: I can't – too dangerous.

FINLAY: You'll be fine.

LEO: I'll be fine now that everyone knows I'm in Glasgow.

MARY: *(Singing to the tune of a Johnny Cash song.)* I walk the line, and she'll be fine.

FINLAY: I'll go on my own then.

MARY: Aye, go on Sherlock! Sherlock'll solve the case.

LEO: Don't get lost.

GODFATHER: Who's Sherlock?

FINLAY: Look, I'm not a stupid little kid, all right!

LEO: I was only/

FINLAY: / If you were so smart you would have found your granddad by now … but you haven't, have you?

LEO: I …

FINLAY: Well I will – see if I don't! *(Starts to storm off.)*

LEO: Wait!

FINLAY: … What is it?

LEO: … Dumpling ingredients … *(She gets a pen, scribbles on a piece of paper and hands it to FINLAY.)* Here.

FINLAY exits.

GODFATHER: *(Shouting after FINLAY.)* Hey, Sherlock! Get us a six-pack and some Buckies!

SCENE ELEVEN

Music from MARY's party on one side, FINLAY at the music college on the other.

Music segues into the sound of classical instruments tuning up. FINLAY walks as if in a big reception hall. MARY is still dancing on the other side of the stage. FINLAY approaches the MUSIC COLLEGE RECEPTIONIST.

FINLAY: Excuse me, I'm doing a school project about musicians. I need to find out about where one of your old students used to live. But maybe your records don't go back that far. This would be about twenty years ago.

RECEPTIONIST: Twenty years – that's nothing, Our records go back to the 1950s. Earlier in some cases.

FINLAY: Oh good, well this guy was called something Chan. I don't know the exact dates he was here, but he played the cello and/

RECEPTIONIST: /Just a minute, sonny. I didn't say we could divulge any information about anyone.

FINLAY: But I thought/

RECEPTIONIST: /It doesn't matter what you thought – it's the Data Protection Act, see. We can't divulge any information about anyone.

FINLAY: But this man's dead now. It's not like I'm going to stalk him or anything … In any case, it's not him, it's his parents I'm trying to track down. And they weren't even students here, … so, it's not as if you need to protect them or anything.

RECEPTIONIST: That's not the point. The point is the Data Protection Act. It's against the law to/

FINLAY: /To divulge any information about anyone.

RECEPTIONIST: Hmmm … Aye.

FINLAY: Oh. Can I speak to the manager?

RECEPTIONIST: She'll tell you the same thing. It's all to do with the/

FINLAY: /Data Protection Act.

RECEPTIONIST: Aye. *(FINLAY stands there looking dejected.)* There's one thing you could do.

FINLAY: What's that?

RECEPTIONIST: You could write a letter in care of us, and we could forward it.

FINLAY: I see … ach … might be too late by then. *(Starts to leave.)*

RECEPTIONIST: Well, that's what I told the other guy.

FINLAY: What other guy?

RECEPTIONIST: We had another fella in here and he was asking the same question as you … about this Chan student.

Was it your teacher, maybe? No, I think he said he was some kind of relation. He didn't look Chinese, mind.

FINLAY: What did he look like?

RECEPTIONIST: I can't remember to be honest– except for the glasses. Very thick glasses …

FINLAY: Oh shit!

FINLAY runs off.

Back at Mary's flat. The party is still going on.

MARY: Leo! It's time for the banquet!
It's time for the bash.
You and me and Johnny Cash.

Cash, cash, lots of cash.
Where is it?
Where's the cash?
Someone's hidden it.
It's under the pillows. It's under the sofa.

Get up, hen! They've hidden the cash.
They've hidden the money for the banquet.

LEO: Mary, what are you … ?

LORRAINE: *(To LEO.)* Gie us a loan of a few quid, hen.

MARY: It's no there. They've taken it.
That Lorraine, she's taken it.
That big-mouth, that long-tongue liar.

Liar, liar, long-tongue liar,
Tell the lads her tongue's on fire.

LORRAINE: *(To LEO.)* Come on, hen, you're a celebrity … gie us a loan … just a few quid …

LEO: *(Ignoring LORRAINE.)* Mary, calm down will you.

MARY: No, I didnae spend it.

No, I'll no go to sleep.
We're celebrating!

LEO: Mary …

LORRAINE: *(To LEO.)* I was talking to you!

MARY: Jammie Dodgers and cornflakes … that's what we need. Where's that salad bowl? We're making cornflake salad. Dumplings – that's what we need.

LORRAINE: *(To LEO.)* Don't ignore me … you stuck up wee cow.

MARY: Leo hen, make some more of they dumplings.

> They dumplings were fit for a king.

> Macbeth! We'll feed Macbeth. We'll feed the King of Scotland.

Banging sound on door.

DRESSING GOWN: *(From behind door.)* TURN IT DOWN WILL YOU!!

MARY: No, I'll no turn it down, Dressing Gown!

> Turn up Johnny! Turn up the cash! Turn up the cushions.

LEO: *(Now distressed.)* Mary, please.

GODFATHER: *(Coming out of toilet.)* That toilet pan's blocked Mary … stinking in there … *(Wipes hands on his trousers.)*

MARY: *(Grabbing LEO.)* Dance, hen. Dance, Leo hen!

LEO resists.

GODFATHER: Allow me … *(He takes MARY and LEO by their wasists and starts dancing round. MARY falls over and GODFATHER pulls LEO closer to him to dance.)* There we go, a girl on each arm.

LEO: Get off me.

MARY: Leave the lassie alone.

GODFATHER: Shut it you, Mary! Just a bit of a dance … me and the wee dumpling.

LEO starts to get upset.

LEO: Get off me! *(Runs out of the flat.)*

MARY: Leo hen, there's nae harm in him.

LORRAINE: Gie us a drink will you, Mary?

GODFATHER: Mary's a naughty girl – aren't you, Mary.

LORRAINE: Mary's got the stash hidden somewhere, haven't you darling?

LEO starts running. She and FINLAY are running at the same time.

RAB: Where's that bleeding paper boy? Another one hit the dust!

FINLAY'S MUM: Come back right now, Finlay!

Running on the spot. MAN IN STREET in darkness.

MAN IN STREET: *(In darkness. Both FINLAY and LEO react.)* Hey, you!

FINLAY and LEO both freeze.

MAN IN STREET: I want to talk to you.

FINLAY starts to move again. LEO runs.

MAN IN STREET: Wait a minute!

LEO: Run, run.

MAN IN STREET: Wait!

LEO: Run – but not on the cracks.

She runs on the spot, then ducks as if to hide. The MAN approaches out of the darkness.

LEO: Walk on past!

MAN IN STREET: What do you think you're doing?

FINLAY: *(To MAN.)* What do you want? *(Points to newspaper in MAN's hand.)* That's not her.

MAN IN STREET: Don't talk rubbish. I saw you put it through the letter box, don't you ever get the message?

FINLAY: What message?

MAN IN STREET: I'm not taking the *Herald* any more. I've left two messages on the answer phone. And tell that Rab of yours I don't want to see it on my bill.

SCENE TWELVE

UNCLE JOHN with birds on one side, LEO on the other. MARY now slumped in her flat with the party still going.

LEO: *(Sighs.)* I'd better go back. I'll go through the park.
It looks different from when I sketched it. *(Sits on park bench.)*
This is where I first met Mary.

UNCLE JOHN: *(To bird.)* Who's got a nice soft neck then?
Who's got a nice soft chest then?

LEO: Finlay still thinks he can track down my grandparents.
Music college – fat chance …

UNCLE JOHN: We're still waiting. We're waiting for that letter.
Are you waiting too?

LEO: It's so quiet here … Except for the birds *(UNCLE JOHN attends to the birds.)* Now they've stopped. If I stop there'll be silence. Lovely, lovely silence.

Silence.

UNCLE JOHN: Don't worry, Daddy's going to open the door.
That's right, out you come.

LEO: Might as well go back … Please let her be asleep …
(Starts to walk.) I can still hear something. Someone's walking along behind me.

UNCLE JOHN: *(To the birds.)* Have a fly around. It's nice to fly around, isn't it?

LEO: *(Starts running again and then checks herself.)* Don't run, and don't look round. Just walk normally – but don't tread on the cracks. If you don't tread on the cracks it will be all right, it will only be someone going to work or to the shops. If you tread on a crack, it could be him.

SCENE THIRTEEN

Split stage: MARY on one side, FINLAY in Chinatown on the other.

Stylised sequence: FINLAY is wandering around as UNCLE JOHN lurks. LEO is still out in the dark. Party in MARY's flat continues simultaneously – dance music is in the background.

FINLAY: *(As he walks around reading from the ingredients list and also approaching passers-by.)* Bok choi, leafy kind ... Is your name Chan? Half cake tofu ... I'm looking for a Mr Chan ... Dim Sum wrappers, Garlic, Ginger ... Chan? Five-spice powder, Sesame oil ... Are you Mrs Chan? ... Soy sauce Spring onions ... Do you know any Chans?

LEO: What am I going to do about Finlay?

FINLAY: Prawns ...

Approaches Old Chinese Woman in a corner.

Excuse me, are you Mrs Chan ... or Miss Chan?

OLD CHINESE WOMAN: No, Chan top floor. Flat 3/2. But not in.

FINLAY: Do you know them – the Chans?

OLD CHINESE WOMAN: Yes, I know them. Mrs Chan my sister. If you want I can give message.

FINLAY: Thank you. Er ... have they lived here a long time?

OLD CHINESE WOMAN: My sister husband come in 1970. Come from Hong Kong.

FINLAY: And do they have any children?

OLD CHINESE WOMAN: No, no children. What is message please?

FINLAY: Oh, that's all right. There's no message. I think it's the wrong family.

OLD CHINESE WOMAN: That is not a problem.

LEO now outside flat.

LEO: What am I going to do about Mary?

FINLAY comes across OLD CHINESE MAN at a still.

OLD CHINESE MAN: Is Asian pennywort.

FINLAY: What?

OLD CHINESE MAN: Good for bladder. Make into tea.

FINLAY: Is your name Chan?

OLD CHINESE MAN: Bladder will be very strong.

FINLAY: No thanks.

OLD CHINESE MAN: Also liver. Use just a little.

LEO: *(Entering flat.)* What am I going to do about me?

MARY: Leo hen!

SCENE FOURTEEN

MARINA and FINLAY are setting up their Saturday market stall.

MARINA: Doughnuts – five for a pound! … *(Pause.)* We need a new savoury line, Finlay. Fancy doing some research?

FINLAY: *(Exasperated look.)* Christ, what do you think I've been doing?

MARINA: Eh?

FINLAY: Nothing – I'll have a wander.

KIM enters.

KIM: *(To imaginary public.)* Try some Dim Sum … Genuine Chinese family food like in China … *(Sees FINLAY.)* Dumplings – free tastes. *(KIM offers FINLAY dumpling to eat.)*

FINLAY: *(Eating.)* I've had these before. My friend makes them.

KIM: But not in Glasgow, I don't think, not the same as this.

FINLAY: Why not … why couldn't she make the same as this?

KIM: –It's a special recipe from my village.

FINLAY: I think my friend uses dough from a packet – these are better. Why did you think my friend's dumplings wouldn't taste like this?

KIM: Well, Dim Sum is a special kind of cooking. Not many people do it in their homes – usually it's just in restaurants. And there's not many Dim Sum restaurants in Glasgow. My parents used to own one, but it closed down. I don't think another restaurant would do this flavour –

FINLAY: Would you mind telling me your name?

KIM: Why?

FINLAY: Please.

KIM: I'm Kim.

FINLAY: No, I mean your surname.

KIM: Why do you want to know my surname? Too many questions.

FINLAY: Look, I can explain.

KIM: Ah, I know, you want to look me up in the telephone book! I think you're a bit young for me. *(FINLAY looks fed up.)* … Okay, my surname is Yeung.

FINLAY: Oh. *(Dejected.)*

KIM: Never mind. You're a nice boy – I'm sure you'll find a good woman. *(She starts to leave.)*

FINLAY: Hang on – what about your parents? Did they have a different name from you?

KIM: My *parents!* My mum would definitely be too old for you. You're such a funny boy! Okay … Yes, my mum and dad do have a different surname. But why do you want to know?

FINLAY: Please just tell me – I'll explain afterwards.

KIM: All right. It's not a secret anyway. They're called Mr and Mrs Mo.

FINLAY: Okay. Well, sorry to bother you. The dumpling things are really good anyway. *(He walks away.)*

Lights up on UNCLE JOHN standing by his birds reading letter.

GRANDFATHER'S VOICE:

Dear Mr Baldwin.

Thank you for your letter. A social worker from the Glasgow Centre for the Chinese Elderly is helping me to write this reply, as I am not very good at writing or reading English.

You are right that my son Matthew stopped being my son when he chose to live together with the English woman you mention in your letter. I did not know they had a child. This child has not been to my house.

Yours sincerely.

Chan Jing

KIM: *(Goes up to FINLAY again.)* Hey … boy!

FINLAY: What is it?

KIM: All these questions just now. Why you so interested in my parents? You work for immigration or something?

FINLAY: Just trying to track someone down, that's all. My friend's grandparents run a restaurant too, or they used to do. But they're not called Mo. Their name is Chan.

KIM: Oh … Well … maybe they are related then.

FINLAY: You said/

KIM: /Chan's my uncle's name – my mum's brother. He was the one who started the restaurant, back in the sixties.

FINLAY: Do you know if he had a son?

KIM: Yes, he did. But he doesn't like to talk about him. There was some family feud or something, and the son moved away. –Why, does that fit in with your friend's story?

FINLAY: Er …

KIM: Your Chinese cook friend. Is she Chinese? Does she go to your school?

FINLAY: Not exactly … but it definitely fits in, yeah … you got a number she can ring?

In MARY's flat.

MARY: *(Suddenly staring out.)*

> Look in the mirror, what do you see?
> One two three, I see me!
> Turn it round, it's unlucky. Turn it to the wall.
> Help me, hen! Help me, Leo hen!

LEO comforts her.

MARINA: *(Calls over.)* Finlay! Well then? What's it to be?

FINLAY: Sorry?

MARINA: What's our new savoury line going to be?

FINLAY: Oh that … er … how about chips? … But not with curry sauce! Someone's doing that already.

MARINA: Aye, we don't want to end up knifed by a rival gang. How about chip butties?

FINLAY: Great idea, Marina. Look, got to go. *(Rushes off in the same direction as KIM.)*

MARINA: *(Back turned away from FINLAY.)* Or how about deep-fried pizza? *(She turns.)* Finlay? … Where's he gone now?

Split stage visual tableaux: UNCLE JOHN is talking to the birds, FINLAY is running on the spot and LEO is comforting MARY.

UNCLE JOHN: *(To the birds.)* What's the matter? We're all ruffled. We're all upset. Is it because Daddy's going away again? Don't worry. This is the last time. I know the address now. He says she's not there but Daddy doesn't believe him.

SCENE FIFTEEN

MARY's flat on one side, KIM on the other.

Country and Western music vamps up. FINLAY comes into flat.

MARY: Sherlock! The case is solved. Sherlock Holmes is back! Wakey wakey everyone! Rise and shine! Rise and shine and walk the line! Sherlock is back wi' us … It's time for the dancing!

FINLAY: *(To LEO.)* I've got a number for you to ring.

LEO: What? *(Music is loud.)*

FINLAY: I think she's related to you.

LEO: *(Distracted.)* I'm worried about Mary.

FINLAY: Her name's Kim. Here. *(He gets a piece of paper out and dials the number using MARY's phone.)*

KIM, half-lit, answers phone.

FINLAY: *(Handing to LEO.)* It's ringing … here.

KIM: Hello?

LEO: *(To FINLAY.)* Who's this?

FINLAY: Kim – I think she's your relative.

KIM: Hello?

LEO: *(Into phone.)* Oh, hi. Um, is that Kim?

KIM: Who's speaking please?

LEO: I'm … well, I'm a friend of Finlay's. I think he met you at the Barras.

Music plays:

She's a devil woman.

Gonna burn, gonna burn my soul.

KIM: Sorry, I can't hear you very well. That music is very loud.

LEO: Yes, sorry. Mary, can you turn it down?

MARY: We can't turn down the dancing! Only the devil turns down the dancing!

LEO: Could you tell me if we could meet up?

KIM: What? Meet up you say?

Music plays:

I thought I was in heaven
Till I looked into her eyes.
Found my angel woman
Was a devil in disguise.

LEO: Well, maybe there's no point.

KIM: I know who you are now! You're the Chan girl that boy was telling me about.

Music plays:

I took my father's rifle.
Shot her and she fell.
Then I knew my devil woman
Had dragged me down to hell.

KIM: *(Having to shout to be heard.)* Why don't you come round tomorrow? Come to 61 Burn Street.

LEO: *(Also trying to shout above the music.)* Sorry – what was that? Burn Street? What number did you say?

MARY: Don't go, Leo! She's at it! She's devilish! Your woman's devilish!

MARY grabs the phone and tries to put it down. FINLAY then takes phone off her.

FINLAY: What number Burn Street did you say?

MARY: *(Grabs the phone back again.)* Don't ask Sherlock. Sherlock mustnae meet the devil. She's in with that Lorraine – they're in it together. They're at it!

KIM: Sorry – who's this?

MARY: You will be sorry, hen – you leave the lassie alone. *(Puts phone down.)*

> *Music plays:*
>
> *Devil woman*
> *Gonna burn, gonna burn my soul.*
>
> *LEO rushes out of flat.*

FINLAY: *(Shouting after her.)* Leo – wait! We'll try again in a minute!

MARY: Don't give up, Sherlock.

FINLAY: Turn the music down, Mary.

MARY: Aye, turn it down! Turn down the music! *(To GODFATHER who walks in with saucepan full of chocolate Hobnobs.)* Turn down the bed! Turn down the job application!

GODFATHER: *(To FINLAY.)* Aye, nae bother Mary. Day three of the party, wee man … doolally time. *(Shows him Hobnobs.)* Here, treat yersel – they won't kill you.

LORRAINE: *(To MARY.)* I'm aff … nothing here to stay for. Mary, what you done wi' my papers?

MARY: I don't want them! Watch your pockets!

> *LORRAINE exits. MARY feels in her pocket, and pulls out a red hat with a pom-pom on it.*

A crown for the Godfather – our leader! *(Throws the hat to GODFATHER. It lands in the pan of biscuits.)*

GODFATHER: That's my girl, Mary. *(Sits down with the pan and puts the hat on his head.)* Any more Tennant's? A drop of liquid for the wee man here. Looks like he needs it.

FINLAY: Maybe I could have a cup of tea.

MARY: Liquid for Sherlock! Liquid for Sherlock! Up! Up! It's under the cushions! That Lorraine'll no find it there. There's nothing left – nae booze, nae nothing! Up! Up and away!

GODFATHER: *(Getting up very unsteadily.)* Place is officially dry – I declare this party is officially kaput … over and done with. I'm aff. *(To FINLAY.)* You coming wee man? *(He staggers and falls back in the chair then almost immediately falls asleep.)*

MARY: *(Pulling at cushions.)* Here they are!

Ten black bottles, sitting on the wall,

Ten black bottles, sitting in the sofa!

MARY produces a stash of tiny bottles from inside the sofa.

FINLAY: *(Inspecting bottles.)* Nail varnish?

MARY: They're yours, pal. They're your bounty.

FINLAY: 'Black Death' … Thank you, Mary, that's really kind, but …

MARY: The best for the best.

FINLAY: But you shouldn't be spending your money on me. Mary, you're not eating properly.

MARY: All things go full circle.

FINLAY: What do you mean?

MARY: Stand in the middle! *(She places her hands on FINLAY's shoulders and pushes him into the middle of the room … arranges bottles in a circle around his feet.)* It's your satellite!

FINLAY: Look, Mary …

MARY: *(Busying herself with the sofa cushions, rearranging them in an outer circle around the bottles.)* All things go full circle.

FINLAY: *(Unsure what to do.)* How about that tea, Mary?

MARY: That's the brew for us! No the Irn Bru – the tea brew! The leafy, leafy, tea-leafy brew!

FINLAY: You sit down and I'll make it.

MARY: No! I'll make the tea brew! I'll make the Hebrew tea brew!

MARY goes to the kitchen and starts twiddling the knobs of the gas cooker.

FINLAY: What are you doing, Mary? We don't need the gas on.

MARY: We need the rings of fire!

FINLAY: No we don't! It's an electric kettle … I know! You could have a nice lie down. My mum sometimes has a cup of tea in bed in the afternoons – she says it's rejuvenating.

MARY: Rejuvenation! … and jubilation! *(She allows FINLAY to lead her towards somewhere to lie down.)*

MARY: I had to tell them. I had to … *(Starts to cry.)*

FINLAY: Tell who what?

MARY: About the leader. L is for the long-lost leader …

FINLAY: *(Trying to change the subject.)* Remember the rejuvenation.

MARY: Aye, rejubilation. *(Smiling through tears.)*

FINLAY: You don't want your tea to get cold. *(Places a blanket on top of her and hands her her cup of tea. She takes a sip.)* I'm just going to get some more milk for mine … *(Notices GODFATHER asleep.)* Godfather – Wake up!

GODFATHER: Uh? Whasser time?

FINLAY: Half past five.

GODFATHER: Jesus … Must do my shift. Did I tell you I'd got a job, wee man? I've a position in the service industry … on the Tesco trolleys.

FINLAY: I'm worried about Mary.

GODFATHER: Aye, she's away with the fairies. Heid's mince.

FINLAY: I'm worried she might hurt herself or set fire to the flat or something.

GODFATHER: Och, she'll be all right. But she should be having the tablets. Has she not been taking them?

FINLAY: I don't know. What tablets, anyway?

GODFATHER: Carbo-something. She's not very keen.

FINLAY: Should we try and find them?

GODFATHER: Better tell the CPN.

FINLAY: Who's that?

GODFATHER: Work it out wee man ... where's Sherlock gone tae? I'm off ... don't want to get my marching orders after only two days. *(Pause.)* Don't know what to do ... do you, wee soul? *(Pause.)* Don't worry lad ... I'll sort it ... the Godfather! ... I'll call the CPN in a wee while myself.

SCENE SIXTEEN

LEO running on one side, UNCLE JOHN and KIM on other.

LEO: Burn Street ... here we are – but what number? Keep looking ... *(Stops running.)* Don't run, and don't look round. Just walk normally – but don't tread on the cracks. If you tread on a crack, it could be him.

Other side of stage.

UNCLE JOHN: *(At buzzer.)* Hello? Is that Mrs ... er ... it says Yeung on the door bell. Is that right?

KIM: That's right, what do you want?

UNCLE JOHN: I believe a Mr Chan lives here.

KIM: What do you want?

UNCLE JOHN: I'm looking for my niece – Leonora.

KIM: No Leonora living here.

UNCLE JOHN: Leonora Watts-Chan ... She's in a disturbed state – she's looking for her grandfather I believe and I understand from my enquiries that this is his address.

KIM: No Leonora here ... I don't know who you're talking about. I don't know anyone called Leonora.

UNCLE JOHN: Yes, I think you do and I think you know who I am, and I think we both know what the right thing to do is.

KIM: I tell you – no Leonora here.

UNCLE JOHN: That's what she's told you to say, isn't it?

KIM: What do you mean? I don't know this Leonora person.

UNCLE JOHN: Perhaps she's even told you some things about her background which may have misled you. But you do need to understand that my niece is a very vulnerable young person. She was in an extremely emotional state when she was in our care.

KIM: Look, none of this is anything to do with me.

UNCLE JOHN: It's a little late for playing games. Leonora is on the Missing People register. Anyone knowingly harbouring her without notifying the police is committing a criminal offence.

KIM: We're not harbouring anyone. Please go away.

UNCLE: You can tell me. I want to help her. Where can I find her?

KIM: I don't know what you're talking about. Go away please.

SCENE SEVENTEEN

MARY's flat.

SOCIAL WORKER busies about, making notes and looking at pill bottles, while FINLAY watches.

SOCIAL WORKER: *(To FINLAY.)* Who did you say you were?

FINLAY: Mary's ... she's my gran, granny's sister. We could keep an eye on things till she's back from hospital.

SOCIAL WORKER: We?

FINLAY: Well, me really.

SOCIAL WORKER: It's kind of you to offer, but we can't give you access to the flat. In fact, I'm going to have to turf you out.

FINLAY: The ambulance driver said I could stay.

SOCIAL WORKER: When?

FINLAY: When he came to collect her. I'll tell you, if it wasn't for me /

SOCIAL WORKER: / Look, I've got to make sure it's secure before I hand the keys to the council. Is there just the one set of keys?

FINLAY: How should I know?

SOCIAL WORKER: Well, it's just that usually the ambulance drivers wouldn't let anyone who wasn't a resident stay in the flat. I'll take a note of your full name and contact details anyway. Sorry to sound like the police – it's just something I have to do.

Phone rings, KIM on other side of the tage with phone. FINLAY makes a move to pick it up.

SOCIAL WORKER: I'll get that … *(Takes phone.)* Who? Leo? No, there's no Leo here. *(She looks at FINLAY who shrugs.)* I think you must have got the wrong number. *(She starts to put the phone back.)*

KIM: I need to speak with her … she might be in danger.

SOCIAL WORKER: There's no one of that name here. If she's in danger you should call the police.

FINLAY: Er … hang on. *(SOCIAL WORKER looks at FINLAY. He stares at the phone … KIM stares out on the other side.)* Jesus … Leo – sorry … got to go. *(He rushes out.)*

SCENE EIGHTEEN

LEO on her own, peering in darkness.

LEO: All these names … so many flats … *(Stops … hears movement behind her then carries on peering at door names.)* Here's one ... Mrs Yeung ... maybe this is it. *(Stops again and listens ... looks round ... nothing.)* Worth a try ... *(Suddenly she is pulled backward in darkness – UNCLE JOHN appears from nowhere and grabs her arm.)* No!

UNCLE JOHN: *(Holding her arm.)* Leonora, it's all right.

LEO: Let me go!

UNCLE JOHN: *(Speaks softly.)* Don't be a silly girl. You know I won't hurt you ... I've got some sandwiches in the car.

LEO: I don't want them. Go away!

KIM appears at window.

KIM: What's going on down there?

UNCLE JOHN: *(Holding LEO's mouth.)* It's all right – a family matter – go back inside, please.

KIM disappears from the window.

LEO: *(Shouts to the window.)* IT'S NOT ALL RIGHT!

UNCLE JOHN: Shush now ... don't be a silly girl. Look, I haven't done anything to you. I haven't done anything to anyone. And you're not to tell anyone that I have.

LEO: I haven't said anything about you.

UNCLE JOHN: I thought not – you're a good girl aren't you? Let's get to the car. Come on. *(He starts to lead her away.)* Aunt Sarah's worried about you as well, you know – we all are. Look at all the trouble you've caused.

LEO: I didn't want to cause trouble.

UNCLE JOHN: Don't worry. It's all right now ... Clemmy and Lemmy have missed you too. Come on. *(He starts to walk her upstage.)*

FINLAY approaches and LEO turns but UNCLE JOHN sees him also and drags LEO off; hand over mouth; FINLAY walks past ... he hasn't seen them. LEO bites UNCLE JOHN's hand.

LEO: Help me!

FINLAY: Leo!

UNCLE JOHN: Keep away, sonny! This is nothing to do with you.

FINLAY: Get off her. *(He struggles with UNCLE JOHN who pushes him away quite aggressively.)*

UNCLE JOHN: Run away now – your mother will be wondering where you are.

Stand-off between them.

FINLAY: *(Bit daunted.)* I'm going to call the police, Leo.

UNCLE JOHN: I think you'll find they'll not be interested in me – I'm this girl's legal guardian.

FINLAY: You're a dirty old pervert, you mean.

UNCLE JOHN: *(Shocked; turns to LEO.)* What have you been saying?

LEO: Nothing ... I ...

FINLAY suddenly kicks UNCLE JOHN hard on the shins; he yelps in pain and lets LEO go; FINLAY flicks his glasses off his face. UNCLE JOHN on all fours looking for his glasses.

FINLAY: *(To LEO.)* Come on!

LEO: *(Pushing FINLAY away.)* No! I have to find out ... *(Makes towards KIM's door.)*

UNCLE JOHN: Leonora!

KIM steps out of the house.

KIM: Stop! *(She slowly bends down and picks up the glasses and hands them to UNCLE JOHN.)* ... That's enough.

Pause.

UNCLE JOHN: *(Still on ground.)* Thank you, Madam. I'm glad someone is behaving sensibly round here. I am this girl's uncle and/

KIM: /Maybe you are … *(Pause.)* But I think I am her family too and she will come with me. I will sort things now.

UNCLE JOHN: *(Still on all fours.)* Listen, you've no right to/

KIM: *(Holding hand out to LEO.)* /Come.

FINLAY: *(Spits on floor as UNCLE still kneels.)* They'll lock you up … you dirty old/

KIM: / Young boy! *(Pause.)* You go off home now …

FINLAY: Aren't you going to call the police?

KIM: I already have.

> *KIM takes LEO into her house and FINLAY turns and leaves. UNCLE JOHN left alone getting to his feet as lights fade and police siren fades up in the distance.*

SCENE NINETEEN

LEO and KIM on one side, FINLAY on the other.

KIM and LEO are chatting and drinking tea … a relaxing moment.

KIM: I suppose you must have a Chinese name too, Leo?

LEO: Yes. It's nearly the same as my English one – Liu, but no one ever calls me that. Well, my dad used to.

KIM: … And your grandparents were called Chan?

LEO: Yes.

KIM: It's a very common name of course. But it looks like your grandfather is Uncle Jing … my mother's brother … he came from the same village as us. You know, I came over here when I was fifteen – the same age as you … My father came to Britain when I was just a baby.

LEO: By himself?

KIM: Yes … He worked in a restaurant – well, lots of restaurants, in England at first … He used to send us letters and we would collect them from the village shop. Then one day he wrote and said it was time for us all to join him … and off we went to Leeds in Yorkshire.

LEO: How did you end up in Glasgow then?

KIM: That's where your grandfather comes in. He came over about four years after my dad and moved here – his wife went with him.

LEO: My grandmother.

KIM: Yes. They didn't have any children then. It was before your dad was born.

LEO: Did you meet them when you moved?

KIM: No. Not for a while. They were already in Glasgow and of course it was quite a journey from Leeds. But soon your grandparents opened a second restaurant in Glasgow and they asked us to come up to help them run it.

LEO: And did you meet my father?

KIM: No, I never did. By that stage the quarrel had happened, and Uncle Jing and Auntie Mei didn't like to talk about him. I gathered he had gone off with some woman they disapproved of.

LEO: … My mother.

KIM: Er, yes … I'm sorry.

LEO: No, it's all right. And my granny?

KIM: I'm afraid she died four years ago.

LEO: Oh.

KIM: Of course, we didn't have your father's address, to tell him.

LEO: No. *(Pause.)* Is he … is my granddad still alive?

KIM: Yes, he is. Actually, this is his house. But he spends most of his time in the Centre for the Elderly. In the evenings he's at home but he just likes being by himself. He doesn't like other people around – even me …

LEO: Can I go and meet him?

KIM: His English is very poor.

LEO: I can sing him the song Dad taught me … 'The Galloping Horseman'.

SCENE TWENTY

FINLAY sitting doing homework.

FINLAY'S MUM: Finlay … What was that film called – the one you saw last night with Ross?

FINLAY: I already told you – *Black and White*. Look, Mum, I've got to finish my homework.

FINLAY'S MUM: What was it about?

FINLAY: The homework?

FINLAY'S MUM: The film you saw.

FINLAY: It was … about a penguin with superpowers. I don't know why Ross was so keen to see it. It was rubbish.

FINLAY'S MUM: What sort of superpowers did this penguin have?

FINLAY: You know, like … well, stopping global warming and things.

FINLAY'S MUM: That sounds interesting. How did he do that?

FINLAY: He kind of flapped his flippers and … well, it was a bit complicated, I can't really describe it. Anyway, Mum, I can't talk now. I'm trying to write this essay.

FINLAY'S MUM: You don't know, do you? You didn't even see the film.

FINLAY: We did! Well, we saw the beginning, but like I said, it was rubbish, so we went and got a Chinese takeaway instead.

FINLAY'S MUM: That's strange, because according to his mother, Ross didn't go out last night.

FINLAY: Mum! You've been spying on me again!

FINLAY'S MUM: And what am I supposed to do when you won't ever tell me the truth?

FINLAY: I'm fourteen. I'm not a baby. I can't tell you every little thing.

FINLAY'S MUM: Finlay, are you hiding something?

FINLAY: There you go again. Just lay off!

FINLAY'S MUM: Can't you see that we care about you?

FINLAY: You *don't* care about me – you just want to meddle into everything and give me a bad name with all my friends.

FINLAY'S MUM: Just tell me, Finlay! Tell me where you were last night. Tell me the truth for once.

FINLAY: I *did* have a Chinese meal.

FINLAY'S MUM: I said the truth!

FINLAY: See! You don't believe me when I *do* tell the truth. You're always like that! You always think the worst of me! *(He gets up to leave.)*

FINLAY'S MUM: Where are you going now?

FINLAY: I'm going to meet a Chinese girl who makes dumplings and a mad old lady in hospital who buys me 'Black Death' nail varnish … it's okay, you don't have to believe me. *(He storms off.)*

SCENE TWENTY-ONE

LEO meets her GRANDFATHER.

Lights up dimly on the back of a man's head in a chair.

LEO: Did you say who I was?

KIM: No, I just said you were a friend.

They go up to him.

KIM: He's sleeping.

LEO: He's got Dad's face – I was expecting a stranger.

GRANDFATHER stirs, then looks at KIM and smiles. She whispers into his ear in Chinese.

KIM: Shushu ni sunnu lai kanni le. *(Hello Uncle. Here is your granddaughter to see you.)*

GRANDFATHER looks at LEO and then looks away.

LEO: Hello, Grandfather.

GRANDFATHER: *(Shaking his head.)* Haishi!... dai ta zou ba. *(No! ... take her away.)*

Pause.

LEO: Dad told me you taught him this song ... *(She starts to sing the 'Galloping Horsemen' but dries up ... he doesn't move. She turns to KIM.)* Well?

KIM says nothing.

LEO: He doesn't want to know me, does he?

KIM: It's just ... *(LEO starts to run away – visual image similar to the start – running.)*

KIM: Leo! *(LEO stops in her tracks ... she breaks down. KIM holds her.)* It's okay. It's okay. Look, it's the shock, that's all. He's an old man ... he'll come round ...

LEO: I wish he didn't look like Dad. It's Dad I really want to see. I want to talk to him, to shout at him even – Why did you have to quarrel? Why were you so proud? Why couldn't you even speak Chinese with me?

Pause.

LEO: *(To KIM.)* Will you teach me?

KIM: Of course ...

LEO: *(Looks out front.)* Now what? This is the bit I've not planned … I wish my hands would stop shaking.

KIM puts her arm around LEO. They both look out.

Tableaux is joined by UNCLE JOHN with his birds.

UNCLE JOHN: On you hop. That's it … I was only talking to her. Can't get locked up for that … You like it when I talk to you, don't you? Say Clever Clemmy! Yes, you're pretty. You love your Daddy, don't you?

Final visual tableaux, characters all looking out:

UNCLE JOHN is feeding the birds.

MARY is sitting on the side of the bed combing her hair.

FINLAY is sitting alongside her.

KIM is standing with LEO.

End.

Learning
Resources

The following pages provide discussion points for students in the classroom or in the drama studio and explore how the play translated on stage. We ask the author of the novel why she wrote it and the playwright why he adapted it. We also look at some comments on the processes of staging the production by asking questions of the director, the designer, and some cast members from the original pilot and Tron Theatre production.These interviews were conducted during the rehearsal period in 2012-13. We also look at the issues that the play highlights.

These notes have been developed from the resources pack used in conjunction with the tour of the original production and we thank Helen Cadbury for her work on that pack.

From Page to Stage – Who does what?

The Author, Julia Donaldson

As an author of so many children's books and stories, what made you want to write the novel *Running on the Cracks*?

Back in the 90s an educational publisher asked me to write a short play for teenagers. At that stage one of my sons did a paper round, and that set me thinking about a storyline in which a paperboy discovers something suspicious going on in one of the houses he delivers papers to. Musing on this idea, I decided that the mystery could involve a runaway being harboured illegally by someone.

I really liked this idea, but I decided that I would rather use it as the basis of a novel than for the play I'd been asked to write. So I wrote a totally different play, called *Top of the Mops* (which is now included in a collection called *Play Time*.)

Meanwhile the idea for the book about a paperboy and a runaway continued to grow in my head. Eventually I wrote a few chapters and a synopsis, and a publisher then commissioned me to finish the book.

I tried to write the sort of story I enjoy reading myself. I have always loved survival stories, in which the main character is out of his or her comfort zone and with hardly any money, having to be resourceful and to form new relationships. I wanted it to be a kind of thriller, so I created Uncle John who is hot on Leo's heels, but I also wanted it to be a book about real people, not just an adventure story.

The Playwright, Andy Arnold

What drew you to the book as a potential stage show and what were the challenges in adapting it?

I had been very familiar with Julia Donaldson's work for younger children as my own children were growing up. I read an interview where she talked about having written a novel for teenagers, *Running on the Cracks*, and I thought it sounded interesting so I bought a copy. I loved it, partly because it is set in Glasgow where I live and partly because Julia writes dialogue in a way that lends itself to stage adaptation. The central theme of a girl running away from home and being pursued by a sinister uncle, together with the relationship between the key characters, Leo, Finlay, and Mary, had the making of a good play in my view.

I decided I would make the play a little darker than the novel. Glasgow would be a terrifying place to arrive in late at night as a runaway, so I have tried to create that feeling. It would have been wonderful to populate Mary's flat with all her friends, but the cast size only allows for Lorraine and The Godfather. I also chose to make The Godfather shadier, especially in how he relates to Leo. Also Jacqueline (from the book) has been absorbed into Kim and actors double up to play other characters. One of the most important choices was to leave the ending more open than in the novel because theatre works differently to fiction. I would like a theatre audience to go away thinking and asking questions about what they've seen.

The Director, Katie Posner

What drew you to the book and to the idea of staging it as a play?

I was interested to find that Julia Donaldson had written this book for older teenagers and I wanted to hear her voice for that age group. The themes and issues of the book are quite hard-hitting and she deals with them in an interesting and insightful way. That drew me in and made me begin to think about how we could explore those themes through Andy's stage adaptation. The other thing that grabbed me was that the characters were so likeable.

Finlay for example, is called Sherlock Holmes. I love the idea of him being this curious kid, trying to make connections. I guess I was like that too at his age. The play mainly focuses on Leo's story, and everything happens around her, but Finlay is the one who is making things happen. He helps Leo and finds the links to her family. With Mary he is really sensitive, which is not necessarily what people expect of a young lad of his age especially as Mary has some mental health problems. I'm not sure how well the issue of mental health is made aware and how much information is made available to young people, but I think everyone will have a different response depending on their own experience and knowledge. It's not really a play that sets out to be about mental health *per se*, it is just that one of the characters is dealing with those issues.

Meet the Actors 1

Suni La
who played many parts, including Kim

Gaylie Runciman
whose main part was Mary

How did the rehearsal process begin?

Gaylie: The process in week one was to walk through it. There are so many characters, so it was necessary to get clarity. It also became clear that there might need to be changes. You sometimes realised: 'I can't be that character because I'll be talking to myself'.

Suni: Or we were finding that we didn't have time to switch from one character to another. It was about ironing out those practical problems, finding the framework of how the whole play moves. By the second week there was more clarity and we were able to go into even more detail.

Gaylie: What was great was that Katie put it on its feet immediately. There wasn't a lot of sitting and talking around a table. We did the first read-through sitting down and then we were on our feet, after a few games and tongue twisters and a ballgame to help us to get to know each other.

Suni: Yes, it was good to make a start without over-analysing it, or each other. We didn't sit around introducing ourselves. It was better just to get up and do something.

Gaylie: Yes, and work as a team, straight away. By Friday we'd walked through the whole play, which was great.

The set was installed in the rehearsal room in the second week. Was that helpful?

Suni: It made a big difference because of working on the different levels. We hadn't realised it would be so high!

Gaylie: It was very helpful to get it so early because it put definition on what we'd already done. It gave us another layer.

Is it different working on a play that has been adapted from a novel?

Suni: It's lovely to have the book to base your character on because you've got the backstory. A lot of the characters come in and out quite quickly in the play, whereas in the book there's a lot more to them.

Gaylie: Sometimes, in the play, two or three characters have been rolled into one, so if you look at the book you can find out about the different aspects of that character.

Is there any advice you'd give someone going into acting?

Gaylie: Well, I never went to drama school. I got turned down everywhere because I was terribly shy and I found auditions terrifying. But I got my Equity Card doing a stage circus and I did an Acting ASM job, then I saved up money and went to a voice coach. Then I wrote about a million letters and I started to get work professionally. So, keep going, and keep working at it!

Suni: I've been out of drama school for four years now. Things I wish I'd known? At the beginning I think you can be scared of going wrong. I wish I'd been braver and realised that in the rehearsal room you can try things out, not be afraid of making mistakes. Especially when you're playing lots of different characters, it's about not being afraid to look a bit silly but just to try things out. If it doesn't work, don't worry, take what does work. The character in the scene we've just been doing, Dressing Gown, I'm trying things out with her. I don't want to make her a caricature, but she can't be too small and naturalistic.

Meet the Actors 2

**Grant
McDonald**
who played Finlay

**Jessica
Henwick**
who played Leo

**Stephen
Clyde**
who played Uncle John
and many other characters

Jessica, you play Leo in the show. Do you identify with Leo's character at all?

Jessica: Definitely. I feel like the journey she goes on is about her coming to grips with her Chinese heritage. Any British born Chinese person goes through this at some stage or another.

I went through that journey when I was about sixteen and I went to the Far-East for three months and completely immersed myself in the culture.

How did you get involved in acting as a career?

Jessica: I started doing LAMDA exams at quite a young age and then I went to the National Youth Theatre and Redbridge Theatre School. After one year, I was booked for my first professional role on the BBC, which was *Spirit Warriors.* That took me out of college for four months and then I just carried on working and here I am!

Grant, as an adult actor you are playing a very young teenager. Do you find it difficult to get inside Finlay's character?

Grant: As a twenty-year-old I find it harder than I expected it to be to play a young teenager. My problem is trying to lighten my tone, and my body language.

But Katie is did a lot to encourage me and highlighted what I needed to do to represent the age more accurately.

Is he a character that interests you?

Grant: I love playing the part of Finlay! He is a Glasgow boy like myself, and I love his energy. The values he has, and his sense of right and wrong, make him a joy to play. I also love the relationships he has with Mary and Leo, and the chemistry we share on stage.

How did you get to this stage in your acting career?

Grant: Well, I'm still currently at college. This is only my second job. I did a job in 2011 and then had my first experience as an actor of not getting work for over a year! And then this came literally out of nowhere. I just got asked to audition one night when I was at a Tron Young Company session – that's a slightly older youth theatre group. I went for the audition and got a phone call a couple of days later saying that I'd got it.

Suddenly doing it in a professional show is strange because there's the familiarity of the place and then I realise I've made that step up. It's quite exciting!

Stephen, what are the challenges for you as an actor in *Running on the Cracks*?

Stephen: Coming up with lots of different accents! I'm from Glasgow but when I was young, because of my dad's job, we moved from place to place, so I lived both South and North of the border, although I've lived most of my life in Scotland. Children are very good at picking up accents. As a child, I liked mucking around and trying out different voices and I always had great fun doing that.

Would you like to be an actor?

Why do you think some actors get lots of work and others don't?

What particular skills are needed when playing lots of different parts in a play?

The Set Design

One of the actors mentioned the set and how high some of the levels were. For a play like this which has many locations, set design is all important.

Here's Gem Greaves, the designer for *Running on the Cracks*.

What was your starting point for the design?

In my initial meetings with director Katie Posner we spoke of an idea of a set which was like play apparatus, a useable framework which would enable the actors to run around, climb, pull things out, spin them around, and keep the fast paced energy of the play flowing, without the need to carry on too many extra props or set pieces. The configuration of the platforms allows different areas to be isolated by the lighting design, closing in the space for intimacy, for example in Mary's flat, then opening back up quickly, by lighting the higher levels.

This will enable the narrative to move easily from one scene to the next.

How has the set developed, with touring in mind?

I created a space which is practical for both the needs of a touring production and the needs of the play, for instance: a certain size for transportation, easy to assemble, designed to fit the smallest venue of the tour, as well as the largest and all the others in-between, then giving the actors different playing areas, height and structure.

What were your influences when designing this set?

Central to the design is the industrial, rusty structure made up of old girders. In our creative meetings we discussed the need to include an element reminiscent of the gateway to the Barras Market in Glasgow. This inspired the design of the structure, along with the influence of ancient Chinese gateways as a nod to Leo's heritage. The steel girders represent Leo's long journey by train with the trusses based on the amazing roof of Glasgow central station, where Leo first arrives in Scotland. The bars of the framework create a sort of cage to the central raised area in which Uncle John can stand and pet his canaries inside their birdcage. Thus the shape of the structure creates a nice frame for many different moments in the play.

If you were going to design the set for this play what would you want it to look like? Have a go at sketching a design – bearing in mind all the locations where the action takes place: the newsagent, the park, the train station, Mary's flat, the market stall, and so on.

Think about how much detail you actually need to convey each space. Why do you think a play needs a set? Could this play be performed in an empty space for example?

Marketing

Every theatre production needs an audience! With a new and unknown play it is especially important to convey what the play is about and try to influence people to come and see it. Here is the image used on the publicity posters and fliers for the original production together with the description of the play:

Run. Keep running. You're doing the right thing. Lie low. Head down. Don't look back. Just keep running, but whatever you do don't tread on the cracks ...
Leo's world has been turned upside down. With her parents gone and a creepy uncle becoming too close for comfort she's certainly sure of one thing ... she must get out. Leo's on the run. She knows what she's running from. Problem is where is she running to?

Adapted from the novel of the same name by the acclaimed writer Julia Donaldson, Running on the Cracks is a fast-moving play about runaways, identity, survival and how friendships can develop in the strangest situations.

What does the image in the poster convey to you?

Does it tell a story at all?

Having read the play, why not try and design your own image for the poster and write your own copy. You have to say everything you want to using no more than 100 words!

Acting Scenes from the Play

Why don't you look at a few scenes from the play and try acting them out.

Have a look at Scene Two, pages 12 to 15. This scene is an example of two pieces of action happening on either side of the stage, at the same time. Finlay is getting his newspapers from the newsagent and rushing round delivering them and Leo is starting on her journey of running away to Glasgow.

Try acting this scene out and see how you get on. Appoint a director to organise the staging.

Another example of the stage being split between two sets of action is Scene Five from page 21 to the bottom of page 24. On the one side Leo is having her first meeting with Mary on the park bench, and on another part of the stage Finlay is making a phone call to Missing People. The two conversations dovetail at times. The trick is for the dialogue to flow as if it is all one conversation. It requires a lot of concentration on the part of the actors. Each actor has to listen to one conversation while keeping focused on the moment that he or she is in the other conversation.

It's always interesting to see how characters change and develop during the course of a play. Look at the way Finlay behaves during Scene Seven in the dialogue on pages 33 and 34 when he first confronts Leo at Mary's flat and is in pursuit of his reward. Then go to Scene Fifteen from page 56 to the end of the scene on page 59. Now we see Finlay trying to cope with Mary's strange behaviour and seeking advice from Godfather during the tail end of the party in Mary's flat.

Choose a character each and act it out. Discuss what is happening with each character.

Why do you think Mary is behaving like she is?

Look how much Finlay's behaviour has changed from his hot-headedness in the first of these two scenes to his conciliatory and more mature nature in the second. Why do you think that is?

Finally, have a look at one of the key issues in the play – a teenager running away from her new home to a strange city at the other end of the country. She has no money and no idea as to where she might end up.

Why not try acting out the parts of Mary and Leo from the beginning of Scene Seven on page 30 through to the arrival of Finlay a short way down page 32. Then discuss what's been said in that conversation. Leo explains what was happening in her uncle's house when her uncle brought her cups of tea in the morning.

Did she do the right thing in running away in search of her Chinese grandparents? Were there alternative courses of action for Leo?

If you had been a friend of Leo in that situation what advice would you have given her?

Discussion Topics and Further Research

Having read the play, you might like to think further about some of the issues it raises.

Running Away and Homelessness

Discuss the reasons why Leo ran away, and then consider other reasons why a young person might want to leave home, and what might happen to them. Students could divide into groups, each group creating a dramatic scene involving a character who either wants to run away or has done so. Then the rest of the class could question and counsel the runaway in each scene.

You could also create an information booklet or poster, giving advice to a young person who is having problems at home.

Below is some information from four charities to get you started.

Railway Children is an international charity working with children alone and at risk on the streets in the UK, India and East Africa. In their own words:

Every year in the UK over 100,000 children under 16 run away from home or care. 30% of these are age 12 or younger, and one in six will sleep rough or with someone they have just met. Some run away or are forced to leave homes where violence, abuse, and neglect have become part of their daily lives. Others run to escape common problems such as bullying and family breakdown.

The problems children face on the streets are often worse than those they were running away from in the first place. Violence, sexual abuse and exploitation are common. Drugs often become an escape from the horrific daily realities of life. Many people assume that there isn't an issue in the UK, but the problems that lead to children running away and ending up on the streets can affect anyone.

ChildLine is a charity providing free and confidential help for young people in the UK. They have supplied the following questions and answers:

I feel like running away is my only option. What can I do?

You might feel there's nowhere else to turn, but running away to live on the streets is never the answer. Sometimes it can help to talk things through with someone else first. This could be a parent or other family member, a teacher, a care worker or social worker.

If you can't talk to someone, or feel that they won't listen, you can contact ChildLine on 0800 1111. Talking to us about what is wrong can help you find a way of solving the problem, before it gets so bad that you run away. We are here for you 24 hours a day, seven days a week and it's free to call, even from a mobile. If it's easier, you can talk to us on 1-2-1 chat at www.childline.org.uk or over email. We won't judge you or tell you what to do, but we will work with you to try to keep you safe.

What can I do if I am homeless?

Being homeless means not having somewhere to live, either because you have been kicked out of home or have run away and feel you cannot return. Many homeless children:

- are forced to sleep on the street, which is not safe and can only be temporary
- get friends to lend them a bed or sofa for the night, which could be dangerous, against the law, or get the friend into trouble
- stay with another family member temporarily.

If you're in any of these situations, you'll be considered homeless by law. The authorities have to act to make sure that you have a safe home, so it's really important to find out what your options are. As a first step it can often be really helpful to talk to a ChildLine counsellor. They will work with you to understand your situation, and to find the safest option for you.

You may be able to stay with another family member on a long-term basis if that family member is able to look after you. This could happen if your parents or carers agree it is the best option.

If you think your parents wouldn't agree to you moving to another family member's home, it might be a good idea to contact social services and let them know what's been happening. They can help you think about your options.

Missing People is a UK charity that works with young runaways, missing and unidentified people, and their families. They operate the **Runaway Helpline**, and here's what they have to say:

Whatever you tell us at Runaway Helpline, we'll listen and offer support. Not judge or tell you what to do. It's your call. You can contact us whenever you want us and however you want. We are here for you.

Runaway Helpline is free, confidential and 24/7:

- Call or text 116 000
- Email 116000@runawayhelpline.org.uk
- www.runawayhelpline.org.uk

You can text us even if you have no credit left on your mobile phone. We will talk to you in confidence to explain your options and try to get you the help you want.

We can't trace your calls, emails or texts.

The Children's Society is another charity that helps to protect young runaways. They produce a series of guides for children, carers and professionals which can be found on their website www.childrenssociety.org.uk.

Further educational materials for ages 9-16 can be downloaded from www.railwaychildren.org.uk/education. These resources, which have been awarded the PSHE Quality Mark, use a variety of methods – including a hot-seating activity and a quiz – to help young people understand the risks of running away, and identify safer alternatives and people who may be able to help them.

Mental Health Awareness

One of the most likeable characters in the play is Mary, the older woman who befriends and shelters Leo. Mary suffers from bi-polar disorder. The novel *Running on the Cracks* won the Nasen Inclusive Children's Book Award in 2009 for Julia Donaldson's depiction of this character.

Read and discuss the following two statements from members of the Pilot Theatre team about Mary and her relationship with Leo and Finlay.

Gaylie Runciman (playing Mary)

Mary is not presented in a way that we just pity her. She's wonderful in that she enables Leo and Finlay to develop and find themselves, even though she's got her own problems.

I like the fact that it's not an idealistic characterisation of someone with a mental health problem. There are times when she's really hard to live with!

Katie Posner (Director)

There is something very important about the way Finlay and Leo relate to Mary. They may never have encountered someone living with a mental illness but they don't judge her.

When things get very difficult, Finlay does what he has to do. When Leo finds herself in Mary's world, she is accepted unconditionally and for a while, feels safe. Sometimes we need to remember that being kind and being caring are basic human instincts and that our strengths as people come out in the most surprising ways.

You may want to find out more about bi-polar disorder or about other mental health problems.

Have a look at the website of the charity **Mind**: www.mind.org.uk.

There is a section called "Your stories" where you can read, watch or listen to everyday stories about how people are living with mental health problems.

WWW.OBERONBOOKS.COM

Follow us on www.twitter.com/@oberonbooks
& www.facebook.com/OberonBooksLondon